The Adventures of Luna & Oxlac:
Death of a Goddess

~

Tanya Araiza Ramirez

For my mother ~ my angel in heaven

CHAPTER 1

LUNA

Although, technically, there had been no phone call from Abuela Monze, Luna Rios knew her grandmother would be visiting soon. Luna could hear her grandmother calling to her in a quiet voice in the calmest part of her mind.

She had begun sensing things at a young age. She always had trouble finding words to describe what occurred when she got one of her "feelings." It was a sudden knowing that would come to her; like remembering you'd forgotten to buy milk once you had already left the market.

Luna's parents and younger brother had grown accustomed to her accurate guesses. There was a time when her parents thought her casual premonitions were eerie coincidences, until the day five-year-old Luna announced her baby brother was on the way. Two weeks later a positive pregnancy test proved to Luna's parents she was right, and nine months later chubby Tona was born. From that day on, they knew their daughter had a special gift. Now that Luna was thirteen years of age, she noticed her gift had intensified in feeling and accuracy. Her parents had noticed as well. So, on that particular day when Luna told her father, Luis, that Abuela Monze would be visiting, he fully expected his mother-in-law to appear with her usual bag full of delicious sweet bread.

Abuela Monze's impending visit fell on a day with a chilly spring morning. Luna's house sat on a quiet street lined with identically shaped homes. Colorful pottery sat on Luna's porch and along her family's driveway, causing their house to stand out beautifully. Crystal-like droplets of dew dangled on every blade of grass, creating a shimmering blanket over the lawn. Luis was admiring the picturesque morning when Luna appeared from her bedroom, briskly walking around the house with small pieces of copal incense burning on the abalone shell her grandmother had gifted her. She opened several windows as the deep, musky scent filled each room. Wrapped in a blanket, her father rushed into the kitchen, and eagerly shut the window.

"Can you please stink up the house on a warmer day?" asked Luis as he reached for a bag of Mexican sweet bread. He realized there was only a small piece left and crumpled the bag in defeat.

"Sorry Dad, I'm on a mission. Abuela's coming."

"Really, when did she call?"

"She didn't. I got one of my feelings."

"Yes," her father declared with excitement, "more goodies." He shook the pastry bag with a frown, "I'm all out."

"You know Mom doesn't like you eating all of those sweets."

"Me? You guys have been eating all of my bread. This bag was full last night." He noticed a long feather on the counter. It was turquoise, with bits of bright green and gold.

"Wasn't me," said Luna, distracting Luis from the feather. She opened the back door and set down the smoking abalone shell on a nearby table. She poured a cup of water over the small burning rocks until they turned black and released one last cloud of smoke. Luis stepped out to the yard with Luna, silently pondering the mysterious feather.

"Is that your blue feather on the counter?" he asked.

The blanket was still tightly wrapped around his shoulders. He held on carefully to a cup of coffee. To Luna, the rising steam looked like little white snakes slithering through the crisp air.

"No. It probably belongs to our pet peacock," replied Luna.

"Don't be sassy, young lady."

Luis lifted his coffee mug and stopped mid sip to observe the large orange tree that sat in the middle of their backyard. A few ripe oranges poked out sporadically from among the thick, pointed leaves.

Luna's father disliked the tree and had always wanted it removed, arguing that a playground or swimming pool should take its place. But Luna's mother, Isabel, would not hear of it. She was fiercely protective of the tree.

"Don't you touch my tree," she would warn with eyes sharp like daggers.

Luis stepped closer to the tree just as a few leaves stopped shaking. "Did you see that?" he asked Luna.

Focused on cleaning out the abalone shell, Luna answered absently, "Nope."

"You're not even looking. The leaves were moving, but nothing was there."

Luna turned toward the tree, barely glancing at it. "That's what leaves do, Dad. They blow around in the wind."

"What wind? There is no wind," he declared. "I don't like this tree. It gives me the creeps."

At that moment a dark brown squirrel scrambled down the tree and paused. Luis sipped his coffee and observed the small creature with mild amusement. Normally squirrels were skittish and took quick, uneasy steps around humans, but this squirrel remained fearlessly still, its small black eyes fixed on Luna's father. Suddenly the squirrel ran along the width of the tree in a circle until it reached a large branch and scurried underneath a cluster of leaves. Before Luis could blink, a small bird flew out from underneath the same cluster of leaves.

"Did you see that?" exclaimed Luis. "The squirrel disappeared, and a bird flew out," he said, shaking spilt hot coffee from his hand. Luis looked down at a small object half hidden in the grass.

"What the heck! My bread! I knew it!" he exclaimed in a mix of Spanish and English and rushed into the house. "Family meeting, right now," he ordered.

Isabel was now in the kitchen with Tona. Luna trailed in, failing to contain her laughter.

"You guys have been sneaking my pan dulce. One of you ate it out back trying to be sneaky. I bought a ton for everyone and all you left me was a crumb." He looked at Luna. "It's not funny, you meanie." Now Isabel and Tona joined in on the laughter.

"It's just bread, I'll buy you some more. No one is stealing your treats," Isabel said sweetly.

"Don't blame me, I only ate one piece last night," said Tona.

"Sorry Dad, but I didn't take it either," said Luna.

"Then why was there bread out by the tree?" Luis asked skeptically.

Without a word, Luna's mother walked outside and around the tree, examining the branches closely. She returned and sat down at the kitchen table. Her eyes looked straight ahead, but her mind was in another place.

"What was that about?" Luis asked with an incredulous laugh.

"Mom, are you okay?" Luna asked.

Before Isabel could answer, the doorbell rang. Tona rushed to the door and threw it open in expectation.

His best friend, James, stood at the entryway with his overnight bag and a box sitting at his feet. "What's in the box?" asked Tona, forgetting his manners and leaving James on the porch.

James pushed his glasses higher up the ridge of his nose and asked, "Aren't we going to camp in your backyard and tell ghost stories?"

"Ya, but I told you we already have tents for each of us."

"But I brought a really big tent so we can all fit."

"Are you too scared to sleep in your own tent?" Tona teased playfully.

"Actually, yes I am," James answered sincerely, not grasping the humor.

Tona laughed. James was funny, but not intentionally. Although he was of a more somber disposition than Tona, they were inseparable. Their interest in all things science and the paranormal was the nucleus of their friendship. Luis also had a passion for ghost stories and enjoyed his duty of scaring the boys with spooky tales.

Luis had an impressive collection of stories from around the world from La Llorona of Mexico to the Taotaomonas of Guam.

James remained on the porch. "Why are you still standing there?" asked Tona.

"I'm waiting for you to invite me in. My mom says I have to wait until I'm invited inside."

"But what if you're a vampire?" asked Tona. "That would give you permission to enter my house and suck all our blood."

James adjusted his glasses. "That would be disgusting." He had caught on to the joke this time and they both laughed. Tona stopped and gave James a puzzled look. "Why are you still standing there? Come in. My arm is gonna fall off holding the door open for you."

Luna could hear the boys laughing from her seat in the kitchen. She was grateful for James' overnight visit. It meant she would get her Abuela Monze all to herself.

CHAPTER 2

ABUELA MONZE

Abuela Monze spoke near perfect English, but even so, she preferred to be addressed as "grandma" in her native tongue, so everyone called her *abuela*. Luna looked forward to each visit from Abuela Monze. Her earliest memories were of the sound of her grandmother's smooth voice as she told Luna fables about ancient Mexico. Fighting off sleep, Luna would beg her grandmother for one last story, preferably one with battling gods or witches. "Just one more, abuela, please," Luna would mumble sleepily. Abuela Monze would always save Luna's favorite myth for last. The creation of the moon. Abuela Monze would end the story the same way every time. "Keep this story in your heart," she would whisper, "it is an important reminder for mothers and their children to always be forgiving and loving."

Though it was her favorite, Luna harbored a love/hate relationship with the moon fable. It was a suspenseful piece of mythology, but, in the end, an innocent earth goddess loses her life and her tyrannical daughter's decapitated head becomes the moon. Luna would have preferred less tragedy. She could not understand why her parents allowed Abuela Monze to name her after a beheaded tyrant. Luna especially thought it unfair, because her brother was named after the revered Aztec sun god, Tonatiuh. However, since most people outside of Luna's family had such a difficult time pronouncing his name, everyone called him Tona.

Luna's father had tried to comfort her with the fact that most people would not know her name meant moon in Spanish nor would most be savvy to Aztec mythology. Abuela Monze would tell Luna, "Once you understand the wisdom to be learned from the moon, you will know what your name means." It was not unlike Abuela Monze to be mysterious. There was something mystical about her. During beautiful sunsets she would say things like, "God painted today," and sigh deeply as if she knew an incredible secret she was not allowed to share. If one day Abuela Monze confessed she was the daughter of a fairy queen or Aztec goddess, Luna would not be the least bit surprised.

The day passed quickly as Luna awaited her abuela's arrival. The cold morning gave way to a rather warm afternoon, but as the sun set, spring's cool night air set in. The baby blue sky had deepened into an indigo hue, with an infinite number of stars sprinkled about like tiny holes poked into a dark canvas. The kitchen window was wide open, allowing in the cool evening breeze while the delicious smells and sounds of dinner time escaped into the night, permeating the backyard with rich aromas and laughter. Luna's mother was unusually quiet and kept her gaze fixed on the open window that held a perfect view of the orange tree.

Luis was in the middle of a ghost story about a lost traveler and a mysterious innkeeper. He described how the innkeeper warned the traveler to avoid the rear bedroom for his own safety. "My relative is afflicted with a grotesque condition and has become like a wild animal," said Luis in a low voice, imitating what he imagined a mysterious innkeeper would sound like. He paused for added suspense and whispered, "Later that night, the curious traveler wandered toward the rear bedroom and peered through a hole in the thin screen door, but all he saw was a red light."

Tona sat at the edge of his chair. James listened patiently and occasionally pushed up the frame of his glasses, which kept sliding down his slender face. Luna's attention was half stolen with expectancy for her grandmother, who had not yet arrived. Luis deepened his voice for the finale. "The following morning the traveler left the hotel and was told by a nearby shop owner how the innkeeper's daughter was possessed by a demon and had red eyes."

Luna let out a sharp scream in hopes of startling the boys. James winced in annoyance.

"Do you get it?" Luis asked excitingly. "The red light was her eyes. She was staring back at the traveler through the hole. Isn't that creepy! It's a true story from Japan."

"That's a good one, dad," Tona said, nodding his head approvingly.

"If it is true, it's most likely her allergies had been particularly exacerbated that day," replied James, unshaken by the spooky tale. "You should see my eyes when I forget my antihistamine on a windy day."

"Allergies don't make your eyes glow, Buzz Killington. Her eyes turned red from evil," declared Tona. He turned to his mother and asked, "What did you think, Mom? Wasn't that scary?"

Isabel was about to speak when she noticed two large, strangely shaped feet dangling from the branches of the orange tree, which then quickly moved out of sight. She let out a startled shout, causing everyone at the table to jump. Luis jerked his head toward the window, but saw nothing out of the ordinary in their yard.

"What was that for?" asked Luna, more puzzled than alarmed.

Isabel did her best to appear calm. "The story scared me," she said awkwardly. Everyone, but Luis laughed at her delayed reaction.

"Did you see something strange out there?" he asked suspiciously.

"What do you mean strange?"

"Like something creepy. Or weird."

"Everything is weird and creepy to you," said Isabel. She rose abruptly and began clearing the table. Luis followed Isabel to the kitchen sink. As he helped her with the dishes, he lowered his voice and said, "I'm being serious. This morning I saw a squirrel running up that tree and hide in some leaves. The branches started moving and then out flies a bird. And I think to myself, 'Where is the squirrel?' It never came out."

"It probably jumped off and you didn't realize," said Isabel with her back to everyone.

"No, I would have seen it. It's like the squirrel transformed into the bird."

"Transformed? Come on, really? I'm not one of the kids."

"I'm being serious. It reminded me of the stories I heard in Mexico about shape-shifting witches." Luis waited for her skeptical rebuttal, but Isabel did not respond with the usual brush off, and so an unspoken discomfort began to brew.

"They're not witches, Dad. Abuela says they are animal spirit guides called nahuales," said Luna. Although it was not her debate, she would not allow inaccuracies.

"Well, whatever they are. They are bad," said Luis.

"Please don't talk about that stuff in front of the kids," said Isabel firmly.

"Why are you getting mad?" asked Luis.

"Because I want our kids to be normal. Not believing in witches and spirit guides."

Luna noticed the uncommon tension. She cleared her throat and pointed to the boys with a glance of her eyes. Luis picked up on her subtle request.

Forget what I said, okay? There are no nahuales in our yard," he

said.

"Thank you."

"Party pooper."

"What did you say?" asked Isabel, unamused.

"Nothing. I love you," Luis quickly replied. He kissed Isabel as she glared at him and tried not to smile.

The doorbell rang. "Abuela is here!" Luna blurted as she jumped from the table and raced to answer the door. Tona followed closely behind her.

"Don't open the door until you're sure someone is there," Luis called after them.

"Why?" asked James curiously.

"If there is a knock but no one is there," explained Luis, "then it's a bad spirit trying to sneak in and you're not supposed to open the door."

"I see," said James, satisfied. Although he usually only half-believed Tona's father, James enjoyed Luis' creative imagination.

Luna and Tona crashed into each other at the front door. A short-lived battle ensued as brother and sister fought to turn the doorknob. Luna's taller frame prevailed. She opened the door to Abuela Monze; her petite frame was covered in a colorful, traditional dress from Mexico. A bright pink shawl hung loosely around her shoulders. Abuela Monze's long, wavy hair was a frame of black and gray around her round face. Her big eyes and warm smile immediately incited enthusiastic shouts and zealous hugs from her grandchildren. She held them in a secure embrace, savoring the moment.

Tona grabbed the white bag of sweet bread from his Abuela and ran to the kitchen. Abuela Monze and Luna strolled into the kitchen arm in arm. Luna was a mirror image of her grandmother. Had they been the same age, they would have surely been mistaken for twins. James, ever the polite guest, rose to greet Abuela Monze. She squeezed his cheeks playfully and hugged Isabel and Luis.

"Where is Grandpa?" asked Tona.

"He was tired and stayed home," replied Abuela Monze. "So, what did I get myself into?" she asked, casually changing the subject.

Tona jumped in to answer, "Mom and Dad were arguing."

"About what?" asked Abuela Monze, half-listening while she tasted the remnants of dinner still warm on the stove.

"Nahuales. Dad says he saw one by the orange tree and that they're bad," answered Tona, eager for his grandmother's input. Still picking at food on the stove, Abuela Monze explained, "Nahuales are not bad. They are not good. How they are, depends on how we are. Your spirit is intertwined with your nahual. It is your shadow soul. If you are good, your nahual will be good." She turned to her daughter, Isabel and said in Spanish, "Speaking of nahuales, I have to talk to you in private about something very important."

Monze sniffed the air and turned to Luna. "Thank you for lighting incense my love. We're going to need all the good vibes we can get."

~

After dinner and a dessert of hot chocolate and sweet bread, Luis lead the boys out back to set up the large tent under the orange tree. Luna stood outside her parent's bedroom, pressing her ear against the closed door. She had hoped to discover the topic of her

17

grandmother's secret discussion, but could not make out the hushed, angry voices. Luna's mother and abuela rarely argued, so she knew it had to be something serious. Luna soon abandoned her espionage efforts and went to her room, where she fell asleep waiting for her abuela to recount the usual nighttime fables.

As Luis and the boys continued their spooky tales, they began to hear suspicious sounds from outside the tent. Tona had just finished a ghoulish tale about a witch that traveled into people's homes through their mirrors when they heard a loud snap outside the tent. They all froze, startled by a sound that came from above them in the orange tree. Luis listened closely. It sounded like something large was moving in the tree. An uneasy feeling filled the dimly lit tent. "Let's move it inside guys," said Luis more urgently than he intended. He stepped out cautiously and looked around. The yard was eerily silent. James and Tona ran for the house. Luis made a valiant effort to walk calmly, but the feeling of being followed overtook him and he made a quick leap for the back door.

Luis made sure the boys were settled in Tona's room before retreating to his bedroom, where Isabel was sound asleep. Luis quickly followed her into dreamland. The stillness of night had just settled in the house when the back door unlocked, breaking the silence of the empty kitchen. Abuela Monze had taught her that bad spirits don't like the light, so Luna always insisted the stovetop light be left on all night. The back door opened slowly on its own. A gigantic figure stooped below the door frame and stepped inside. The soft light created just enough illumination to outline the figure in shadow. It entered the kitchen and headed straight for the cake plate with the glass cover, which held Luis' beloved sweet bread. The stranger lifted its enormous hand over the cake plate, and as it did, the glass cover lifted in the air without being touched. In a moment, three of the five pastries were devoured.

The tall stranger stooped under the doorframe and walked down the hallway toward the bedrooms, his soft leather shoes slapping softly on the hardwood floor. As he passed the children's rooms, he reached into a small pouch that hung around his neck and blew a colorful powder at each door. He stopped at the master bedroom. The door opened by the stranger's silent command. The tall figure stooped low to enter the room, disturbing a nearby dresser, which knocked over a large picture frame that crashed to the floor. Luis awoke with a start and quickly turned on the lamp next to his side of the bed. Before he had time to comprehend what he was seeing, a terrified scream escaped his agape mouth. Hunched in the corner of the bedroom was an eight-foot man with long black hair and an impressive headdress, with bright, colorful feathers that brushed against the ceiling. Isabel sat up, jerked from her sleep by Luis' scream. She turned to see the giant, who chuckled to himself, amused by Luis' terrified scream.

Isabel slammed her hand on the bed and firmly said, "Bad Oxlac. Stop that. You're scaring him."

Abuela Monze rushed into the room as if she already knew the cause of the commotion. She immediately turned to Oxlac. "Put him to sleep, you're scaring the poor boy," Monze demanded in the ancient Aztec language, Nahuatl. Oxlac reluctantly reached into his small pouch and blew the powder at Luis, who dropped back into a deep sleep.

Panic immediately set in. "Why is he here? What's wrong?" asked Isabel in earnest. She knew only something severe and precarious could lure Oxlac back to their world. The last time Isabel had seen Oxlac she was ten years old. Monze had just returned from a journey with Oxlac, beaten and barely conscious. Isabel could still remember her father banishing Oxlac from their home as he desperately tried to stop the bleeding from a wound on the side of Monze's face. The last image Isabel had of Oxlac was of his large feet as he ascended the very tree that still stood in their yard.

"He needs me," said Abuela Monze sternly, not meaning for her words to sound so harsh. "I have to go, Isabel. I told you. It's why I came here tonight."

"What if you get hurt again, or worse? What about Dad? Does he know?"

"Yes. He won't speak to me."

Unable to stand the discomfort of the confined space of Isabel's bedroom, Oxlac shifted his position with a loud huff. Without warning, his gigantic frame transformed from a squirrel to a bird and then into an average-size man. He reached out and gently touched Isabel's face. "You are old now," he said with affection as Isabel stepped in to hug him.

"I kept the tree for you, but you never came back," said Isabel with the pain of disappointment.

"Oxlac is always watching. Oxlac always sees you," he replied.

"I told you before, it takes too much energy for him to shift into human form here," Abuela Monze said to Isabel. "Plus, I didn't want to upset your father."

Isabel suddenly realized the connection. "Are you the squirrel? Have you been eating Luis' bread?" Oxlac smiled, pleased at his mischief.

"Why are you here?" Isabel turned to Oxlac, but he turned to Monze to answer.

"Please understand," said Abuela Monze, "the reason I must go with Oxlac is a very important one."

Isabel looked to Oxlac for an explanation. He was just as she remembered him, austere, yet mischievous and playful.

Oxlac finally leaned in closely to Isabel. His words were slow and determined. "The others will heed Monze. And with her magic, no one can truly be harmed. So, it must be. She comes with Oxlac or there will be no moon and the stars will be at war."

With her emotions somewhere between worry and frustration, Isabel turned to her mother and pleaded. "You can't do this, Mom. You could be killed. How can you not be thinking of your family? We need you."

"Mija, when you choose a life of service, you must always be ready to sacrifice for those in need. She'll die if we don't help her. I have to go."

"Who will die?" asked a small voice out of nowhere. Isabel and Monze jumped. Luna stood in the doorway, blinking away sleep from her eyes.

"Luna, go back to bed," Isabel demanded.

Abuela Monze guided Luna into the room and shut the door.

"It's time they met," she said.

Luna saw Oxlac and did a double take.

"WHO THE HECK IS HE?!" she exclaimed.

"He's an old friend," said Abuela Monze.

"Why is he dressed like that?" asked Luna as she tried to process every detail of Oxlac's appearance. Oxlac remained unmoved and observed Luna with a quiet curiosity. He inspected the contents of the small bag that hung on a slender leather rope around his neck. He turned back to Luna and said in broken English, "You are not asleep. Oxlac's magic is superior. Why are you not asleep, little rat?"

22

"I'm not a rat. I'm Luna," she declared. And then asked, "Who is Oxlac?"

"Me."

Luna paused for a moment. She thought to herself, *The only logical explanation for this strange man's presence must be completely illogical,* and so she asked, "Are you the shape-shifter who lives in my tree?"

"It is my door."

"What are you?"

"Whatever I want to be."

"Are you a witch?"

"He's a shaman," interrupted Abuela Monze, "a very special shaman."

Luna observed Oxlac and did not think he looked very special. He could not have been more than fifty years old. He was muscular but very lean; his multicolored jewelry and clothing made him look more outlandish than impressive. He wore a tunic of linen. The collar and belt were covered in beads of every hue. However, Luna had to admit, his headdress was extraordinary. Feathers of every shape and color sprouted from a thick, beaded headband like a colorful waterfall. She noticed that with each small movement of Oxlac's head several feathers fell from his headdress, leaving a pile of glowing turquoise at his feet. Although in just moments he had lost numerous feathers, his headdress remained perfectly intact, as if he had not lost even one.

Luna could have dismissed the stranger's appearance as eccentric had it not been for one detail; half of the man's body was painted like a skeleton. The left side of his body was painted black. Bold white lines meant to look like bones contrasted brightly against the onyx pigment. The other side of his body was painted with several designs of vibrant hues of yellow, blue, and red. Each color gleamed as if just freshly painted. The man looked more strange than special. Her abuela began to explain how Oxlac had the power to bend time and space and travel to different dimensions. He was a powerful healer and magician, called upon in times of need by every being imaginable from every realm imaginable. He could instantly travel back in time to moments that occurred hundreds, even thousands of years earlier on Earth or in some other reality where ancient gods or fairies or other creatures existed.

Luna continued to observe Oxlac as he turned to Monze and said gravely, "She does not have time. We leave now or she will die."

"Who will die?" implored Luna.

Oxlac turned and said a name Luna had heard many times during her grandmother's storytelling.

"Coatlicue," said Oxlac.

CHAPTER 3

COATLICUE

Coatlicue existed during a time when ancient gods in Mexico were not yet ancient. A time when there was no moon, only stars to fill the evening sky. Each night the sun god, Tonatiuh, retreated to journey through the underworld and left the stars to light the sky. The humans on Earth were accustomed to their evening sky in chaos and always had a candle or torch at the ready, for the star gods were a group of numerous temperamental beings. In one moment, the sky would light up in fiery hues of red and blue as the star gods quarreled, illuminating the lands below as bright as day; but in the next moment, they would calm and the sky would fade to near black with only a faint glow of white, and the mortals below would quickly reach to light their candles.

Regardless of the turmoil in their firmament, the humans went about their lives in their Garden of Eden surroundings. The lands were populated with thriving kingdoms with colossal pyramids, lush gardens and sprawling waterways that carried fresh water to the rich and poor. This paradise was home to royal families, workers, peasants, artists, and warriors. Everyone had their place in society and served a specific purpose depending on what class level fate had birthed them into. However, each person shared one thing in common: worship of the gods. In ancient times, they believed the gods controlled everything from the harvest to childbirth. From songs to poems and even human sacrifice, exorbitant praise and devotion were constant requirements to secure a good life.

Artists were paramount to every kingdom. They provided various platforms for the people's idolatry. They could write songs, design temples, or paint murals of godly reverence. Out of all the artists, poets were most esteemed. Their gifted words of praise were powerful enough to rival the ultimate gesture of devotion: sacrifice of a human heart. The fiercest gods were favored by the poets. Although clever, the poems were all the same: countless exaggerations of a god's power.

Coatlicue received little attention from the poets. She was an earth goddess bestowed with the humble duty of sweeping the floors of the great temple in the sky, Coatepec. This temple rested at the end of a long staircase that reached the border of the sky and heavens.

One day, one of the only poets particularly fond of Coatlicue walked through the jungle near his village, inventing clever verses he was obliged to recite to the king. Renowned for his poems at such a young age, he was solely referred to as The Poet. As he came upon a small clearing during his daily walk, he noticed a most unusual sight: white feathers were falling from the sky. Although already a young man of twenty-two, The Poet smiled to himself like a curious child when he saw the feathers dancing against the warm air and landing softly on the earth. The feathers sparkled in the sunlight and had formed a trail to a staircase that had appeared from nowhere. He stood at the first stair and wondered how it was he had never noticed such an obvious structure before. His eyes followed the length of the stairs until they disappeared into the clouds. Born with a bold and curious nature, The Poet ascended the large, white marble stairs without hesitation. By the time he neared the last step, the sun was setting.

When he reached the top, the clouds pulled away to reveal the entrance of a grand temple. Ornate, colorful designs were carved into every inch of the stone structure. Ivy and flowers unlike any he'd ever seen crawled along the temple walls. An orchestra of sweet aromas overwhelmed his senses. Growing up, The Poet had been told many stories of the sacred mountain, Coatepec, but he had not thought it possible for a human to behold it. The Poet stepped inside the large entrance and stood for a moment to allow his eyes to adjust to the dimly lit room. It was pleasantly cool and smelled of incense. The only sound came from the flickering flames of the hanging torches, which were widely dispersed throughout the enormous room, casting an eerie movement of light along the walls.

"Hello," he said cautiously, but there was no reply.

He returned to the entrance where he admired a broad view of the sky and earth below.

The great pyramid of his king stood out proudly among the trees far below. An array of warm, golden colors danced along the treetops as the sun set. The Poet closed his eyes and said to the setting sun, "Safe journey, Tonatiuh. May you return safely in the morning." The Poet could hear the soothing sound of the rivers below as the stars appeared and glimmered in the sky. A myriad of bird calls filled the air in melodic harmony. The Poet had never experienced such beauty, and he understood in that moment why the earth goddess, Coatlicue, had always held a special place in his heart. He could not help but be in complete reverence of her power to create such a magnificent world. "Life without birds, rivers, and mountains would be meaningless," he said to himself.

A poem for Coatlicue sprung from his heart. As a boy he was told the goddess Coatlicue resided in the temple of Coatepec. He hoped the cool winds would carry his words to her and so he said aloud:

Your hair,

A blanket of stars.

Your body,

Rivers running through the brown earth.

My soul is your willing prisoner.

I abdicate my inner being

To melt into the abyss of your light.

I dream of shattering myself into a million pieces,

One of me for each of you.

The Poet reflected on his poem; this was the only way he knew how to describe the beauty of what he imagined was Coatlicue. She was the sky and earth, rivers and trees, grains of sand and beams of starlight.

He sat for a long while, unaware that he was not alone. Coatlicue stood behind a pillar in a far corner of the temple, overwhelmed by the intoxicating words of the mysterious human who had warmed her heart. The gods and goddesses knew of many things: war, anger, power, and delight, but they did not know what it felt like to love. Coatlicue quietly observed The Poet and was disappointed when he rose and descended the staircase. She continued her eternal duty of sweeping the floors of the temple in the sky, but this time with the hope in her heart the man would return.

Over the next few days The Poet felt foolish. Coatlicue was ever present in his mind. He constantly shook her from his thoughts, like an angry dog shaking off water from an unwanted bath. He struggled to comprehend how an earth goddess could imbed herself into his mind. His heart felt such longing for her that it quickly led him into a constant state of agitation. "She is not human," he would tell himself. "You cannot love a goddess as a man loves his wife," he would declare. But he was soon betrayed by his desire as he imagined what it would be like to feel her in his arms.

The Poet found himself back in the jungle where he hoped the staircase would be. Desperate for relief, he hoped that returning to the place that ignited his obsession would ease him. His heart sank at the sight of the ordinary plants and flowers that sat where the staircase should have been. Unsure of what to do, he stood and waited, though he did not know for what. And then they appeared.

Three hummingbirds of the most enchanting shades of pink, green, and blue glided a few inches from his face as if in a playful dance. They flew a few feet in front of him and that is when he noticed the staircase. It was as if the hummingbirds had manifested it.

The Poet climbed the stairs without shame of looking foolish for his clumsy, hurried steps. He felt the hot air cool as he reached the top. Once again, the clouds cleared, revealing the ancient structure.

He stepped into a room with an opening in the ceiling and waited. As he lay on his back and looked up at the glowing sky, the sounds of the jungle below faded away. The flickering of the surrounding torches slowed and the flames swayed gently in a trance-like dance.

Coatlicue hid nearby, awaiting The Poet's voice, her heart beating with excitement at his return.

The Poet whispered to himself:

Coatlicue,

You and I

We are a rhythm in the same heartbeat.

A peaceful torment in your presence

Relief to my soul even unseen in your view,

Relishing in the moments of even

The smallest glimpse of you

There was a noise. The Poet jumped to his feet. He wondered if he could run fast enough to escape. "Don't be frightened," whispered a woman's voice out of the darkness. He noticed a small light appear nearby. The light grew brighter and larger as it approached him, until it became the figure of a woman. The Poet and

Coatlicue stood face to face. He froze, taking in the unearthly beauty of the woman with glowing skin and black hair that sparkled as if painted with stars. He was immediately struck by the intensity of her large, round eyes. Coatlicue reached out to touch The Poet's kind face. He was transfixed and did not pull away.

"Who are you?" was all he could whisper.

"Coatlicue," she said softly.

The Poet closed his eyes as he felt a strange tingling throughout his body from her touch. He leaned in to kiss her. She did not pull away.

~

The Poet awoke dizzy with unawareness of how long he had slept. Coatlicue had led him into a room at the very rear of the temple. They had spent what felt like hours in the elation of each other's affection. The ardent emotions and comfort were such that The Poet felt for sure they were familiar souls that had been reunited.

When The Poet turned to embrace Coatlicue, he realized she was no longer lying next to him. "Coatlicue," he called out in a hushed voice, but there was no answer.

Fighting off the knot of dread in his stomach, he wandered the temple searching for her. There were several rooms that surrounded the main, larger room with the skylight opening. There

32

was also a long, dark hallway that seemed to go nowhere and left The Poet with an uninviting feeling. He decided it was best to avoid it.

The Poet was sure his night with the earth goddess had not been a dream, but he would have preferred the reality that it was only a fantasy rather than the possibility that he had meant nothing to Coatlicue. The voice in his mind told him to give up the foolish effort and leave, but the ache in his heart told him that without Coatlicue it would never be whole again.

The heart can swell with many forms of love. A soul connection is the rarest kind. This love is the most powerful, the most overwhelming and the most joyous. However, if the lovers are divided, then the heart is torn apart, leaving two halves bleeding and painfully wounded.

Therefore, the inner desolation was one The Poet had never felt before. He sat at the entrance of the temple and waited until the next morning.

Coatlicue did not return.

Crestfallen, he walked to the stairs and took slow, sad steps until he reached the jungle floor. Lost in heartache, he did not notice when the staircase vanished as he walked away.

~

Coatlicue knew what would happen to her if she went to The Poet the night he returned to the temple. She knew her betrayal with the human would be discovered and she would be punished accordingly. What she never imagined was there would be a child growing in her belly. A child growing so quickly, she felt it begin to move while she watched The Poet sleep peacefully. Despite the impending calamity, Coatlicue did not regret her night with The Poet. The elation he ignited in her smothered the possibility of repentance.

What shattered her spirit most was realizing no punishment could be as severe as the pain of his absence. Even if she was allowed to live, the humble goddess would never be granted permission to remain with a mortal.

Coatlicue held her belly tight and told herself to stay alive, at least long enough for her child to be born. She knew there would be no mercy from her kind, so, she hid herself, knowing it would only be a matter of time before they found her.

Nothing went unnoticed to her children, the 400 Star Gods; they were keen witnesses to all that transpired below their sky. So it was, as Coatlicue rushed to hide herself deep within the temple, her children plunged from the sky and charged Coatepec. Her daughter, Coyolxauhqui, leader of the 400 Star Gods, stormed through the entrance of the temple.

"Where are you, Mother?" Coyolxauhqui screamed angrily. "You have disgraced us and you must be punished," she seethed.

One of the 400 Star Gods was the last to reach the temple's entrance. His conscience had slowed his pace. Crime or not, he could not harm his mother, and so he abandoned his siblings and flew at the speed of light to find Oxlac.

Oxlac made his way through the jungle as quickly as he could, shape-shifting into various forms until he decided on a small bird. He cut through the surrounding greenery effortlessly, with a large figure looming over head. The trees ended, giving way to a ravine. Oxlac looked back to make sure he was still being followed. A gigantic vulture broke through the tree line and continued closely to Oxlac. A fearsome creature rode on the back of the vulture and kept its large red eyes focused on the temple that was now visible through the clouds.

Coatlicue was soon discovered in her hiding place by her children. She was dragged to the center of the temple and thrown at the feet of her daughter, Coyolxauhqui. The sun shone through the skylight, blinding the frightened earth goddess with its golden beams. A huge shadow appeared from above. The great vulture descended upon the temple. The warrior goddess, Itzpapalotl, jumped from the vulture and landed between Coatlicue and her angry mob.

Itzpapalotl's massive figure loomed over the smaller 400 Star Gods. With each step her clawed feet made a menacing scratching sound against the stone floor. Black feathers hung from her red and yellow painted body; her butterfly shaped wings were edged with obsidian knives. Her square face was painted red and white, with skeleton-like teeth protruding from her face.

Itzpapalotl approached Coyolxauhqui and hissed, "It is forbidden to harm a mother with a child in her belly. Leave now or you will know that I am Itzpapalotl."

The 400 Star Gods remained silent as their leader leaned in to meet Itzpapalotl's glare as she said, "You leave now or you will know that I am Coyolxauhqui."

Oxlac transformed into his human shape and calmly stepped forward. "Do your best, Itzpa, and trust that I will be back with help."

Itzpapalotl nodded and reached out her sharp fingers. In a blink, Oxlac was a squirrel jumping into Itzpapalotl's grasp. She hurled Oxlac up toward the skylight as he became a hummingbird and made his escape just as the violence began. Oxlac hoped he had enough magic to reach Monze. A dilemma of this magnitude would require the assistance of his old friend.

CHAPTER 4

FREYA

Luna, Isabel, and Abuela Monze listened as Oxlac told the story of Coatlicue. Being a shaman of few words, it did not take him long to summarize the plight of Coatlicue and his own near escape.

"But, how could you have seen all of that and now you are here?" asked Luna. "It happened in the past."

"Simple," replied the shaman as if nothing could be more normal. "I became a bird, escaped the temple and used magic to open a portal. And now Oxlac is here."

Luna could barely process what she was hearing. Only a few minutes had passed since she discovered Oxlac in her parents' bedroom, conversing with her mother and Abuela Monze. Her father lay passed out from the shaman's sleeping dust. Luna tried to rationalize how an otherworldly shaman could be in her house asking for help to rescue a goddess. Luna noticed a soft jingling sound and realized Oxlac had small bells tied around his ankles and wrists. She stepped closer to observe the intricacies of his attire and noticed he smelled of an odd but intoxicating mixture of herbal and musky scents.

Luna could see her mother growing anxious by all of the time travel talk. "But how can you save her, if all of this already happened thousands of years ago?" asked, Isabel, annoyed by the impossibility of it. "I know this story. Coatlicue dies, her daughter is killed and becomes the moon. You can't save her, so my mother will stay here," said Isabel firmly.

"Coatlicue will not die," insisted Oxlac.

"Mom, tell him. He can't change the past," said Isabel to her mother, Monze.

Oxlac shook his head and said, "In this moment, is this reality, but it can be changed. Time and space are always moving. Time is not like a rock, it is like water. So, when Oxlac is called, he must answer. He must change what is."

"I'm sorry for Coatlicue. It is very sad, but you can't take my mother," said Isabel.

"We can save Coatlicue," said Oxlac.

Luna noticed her mother look out the window at the full moon glowing brightly in the night sky. Luna tugged at her arm. "Mom, we have to let abuela help him. It's not right to let Coatlicue die if we can help. You know how much I hate how unfair her story is. If she was your daughter, wouldn't you want to help her?"

Isabel tried to ignore Luna, but she persisted. "I have one of my feelings, Mom. Abuela is supposed to go. We are supposed to help Oxlac," said Luna earnestly.

The room was heavy with tension until Isabel finally spoke and said, "Just bring my mom back alive."

"Thank you, Isabel," said Oxlac with a grateful bow.

"Can I go?" asked Luna, "I want to help save Coatlicue."

"No," Isabel and Abuela Monze answered in unison.

"But I feel it. I must help Coatlicue. I am supposed to go too, Mom. Don't you believe me?" In the years since Luna had begun having her premonitions, she had never felt one so strong as she did in that moment.

"There is no way you are going. It will be dangerous," said Isabel.

Without a word, Oxlac smiled at Luna and left the room. Abuela Monze kissed Luna warmly on the cheek and said, "Please go back to bed, my love." Luna partly obeyed her grandmother and returned to her bedroom, but she did not go sleep.

Isabel escorted Monze and Oxlac to the kitchen. Before Isabel could say another word to dissuade them, she was blinded by a burst of sparkling particles. Before she could realize that Oxlac had blown his sleeping dust in her face, Isabel was fast asleep. Oxlac carried Isabel to her room and laid her gently next to Luis.

Oxlac and Abuela Monze left quickly before anyone else awoke and tried to stop them. Luna snuck to the kitchen and watched through the window as Oxlac and her Abuela Monze climbed the orange tree and disappeared. Without a second thought, Luna ran out the back door. As she struggled to climb the tree, the force of the portal jerked her up the branches and into a dark tunnel. Her heart raced as she struggled to make out her surroundings as the wild sound of whipping winds disoriented her. Although she had climbed up the tree, it felt as if she were falling, until she was surprised with sudden impact. When Luna lifted her dizzy head, she looked up to see she had landed on soft grass in a beautiful meadow.

Luna observed her surroundings in awe. The sun was shining, with the pleasant sound of birds happily chirping. A sea of colorful flowers filled the meadow; glowing butterflies and hummingbirds zipped by. White, puffy seeds of dandelions were released into the air every time she moved, creating a billowy mist around her. Still dizzy, she struggled to stand. Luna noticed Oxlac and her Abuela Monze crouched behind nearby bushes frantically waving to her. Luna sensed their urgency and ran to the bushes. Oxlac yanked her to the ground and motioned for silence.

"We don't have permission to be here," whispered Abuela Monze urgently.

Across the open field, Luna noticed a bird the size of a car take flight. A giant creature emerged from the forest, towering over the treetops, and snatched the bird in an effortless grasp. Before the bird could release its distress cry, it was down the giant's throat. Abuela Monze covered Luna's mouth to stifle her scream. The creature stopped to listen. Everyone held their breath as it sniffed the air with suspicion. Satisfied no other meals were available, the giant continued on its way.

Abuela Monze could barely contain her anger. "What are you doing here?" she demanded of Luna.

Shaking, Luna stuttered, "What, what was that?"

Oxlac replied without taking his eyes off the meadow. "An ogre. They eat living things."

"You mean animals, right?"

"They prefer humans," replied Oxlac.

Oxlac's reply sent a chill through Luna. "How did it see the bird?" she asked, still processing the unpleasant event. "It didn't have eyes."

Oxlac pointed to his ears and nose. "No need for eyes. They hear and smell better than a lion," he whispered.

"Do you understand now?" said Abuela Monze angrily as she pulled Luna close. "These places are dangerous, Luna. We could be killed."

"Can't you take me back?" Luna asked Oxlac, partly regretting her decision and partly excited she had just traveled to another world.

"Oxlac cannot take you back. The door is closed now," he said matter-of-factly.

"What?" exclaimed Luna.

"Shhh," hissed Abuela Monze.

"Mom and Dad will be so mad when they see I'm gone."

"We will be back before they wake," said Monze.

"Why can't you just open another portal?" asked Luna.

"Not enough magic," said Oxlac, carefully observing their surroundings.

"How do you get more magic?"

Monze took a moment to choose her words before stepping in. "Mija," she said calmly, "this was an unplanned trip for Oxlac. He only had enough magic to reach me and then get us here to see Freya. Oxlac's magic is back at his home. He has very little left with him now and so we must rely on the help of those we seek to get us home."

"Are we going to be eaten?" asked Luna, trembling. The ogre's image was burned in her mind. It was at least a few stories tall and its entire body was covered in flesh that resembled an open wound.

"If we are brave and careful, we will not be eaten. We must try not to be scared," said Abuela Monze as calmly and quietly as possible.

Luna inhaled deeply and said, "I am not scared. I am brave."

"That's right, my love," said Abuela Monze proudly.

"Let's find this lady, Freya, and she will get us home. It can't be too difficult, right?" asked Luna with a hint of doubt.

"The goddess is not always agreeable," said Oxlac.

"Wait, do you mean the Nordic goddess Freya? The real Freya?"

Oxlac nodded yes.

"I'm going to meet Freya," Luna said excitedly to herself.

Distracted in conversation, Luna, Oxlac, and Monze did not notice their presence had been discovered. Without warning, the four of them were lifted into the air by three towering figures dressed like soldiers. Luna and her Abuela screamed as they rose through the air. Oxlac only shrugged his shoulders and sighed calmly at the unfortunate situation. Although not as tall as the ogres, the soldiers were an impressive height, and dangled their captives at their sides as a child would a doll.

A wide creek ran along the edge of the meadow, creating a border between the forest. They stopped at the center of a towering

43

group of trees that stood out from the grove, the trunks in perfect alignment of a half circle. Luna and her fellow travelers were tossed onto the soft grass of the meadow, creating an explosion of fluffy dandelion seeds. Once the cloud of white fluff cleared, Luna could see a woman standing in the shallow creek, playfully dragging the tips of her toes along the surface of the bubbling water. Luna knew immediately the woman was Freya.

Several tiny creatures flew about Freya playfully, which Luna could only guess were faeries. Freya giggled each time one whispered in her ear. Freya turned and smiled at Oxlac. "You've come to my land without invitation, Oxlac." Before Oxlac could speak, Freya said firmly, "You know I do not like that."

Luna was too amazed to be frightened. Freya was easily the most beautiful woman she had ever seen. Her shimmering gown hung softly on her body. Her skin was like glittering porcelain. Luna could not tell if Freya's long hair was gold or red as it appeared to be both at once. As if all of this were not enough, Freya's most stunning feature were her emerald green eyes. Freya touched the necklace of amber stones that rested along her collarbone and looked carefully at each interloper. She approached Oxlac, who'd sat as he landed, and with her bare foot tilted up his chin to face her.

"Why are you here, shaman?" she asked.

Oxlac kissed Freya's foot before moving it from his face and stood up to dust the flowers and fluff from his clothing. "We need your magic," he finally said.

Freya laughed out loud. "Have you not magic of your own, my fellow sorcerer?"

"Strong magic is needed."

Freya's interest was piqued. "Sounds like someone's in a pinch," she giggled.

"Coatlicue faces death. Coyolxauhqui will kill her," said Oxlac.

Male servants emerged from the forest and set out a delicious spread of wine and various fruits and cheeses on a long wooden table. Freya finished a chalice of wine in one gulp. "Why should I help those barbarians? They are no better than my worst enemies here." Freya touched her chest as if in pain. "Only a brute would want to kill her mother. Mothers and children are meant to love. Your star gods are atrocious, Oxlac. Why cannot they be more civil in their violence, like your serpent god?"

Luna stepped forward. "What about Coatlicue and her poet? They are not atrocious. They're in love. Don't you want to help them?"

Freya eyed Luna curiously.

"My grandmother told me," continued Luna, "although you're a very powerful magician, the thing you treasure most is love."

"True," said Freya thoughtfully, "but I'd rather not trouble myself with unnecessary perils over a pair of ill-fated lovers."

A lone hummingbird glided gracefully through the air to Freya. As it hovered to greet the goddess, the rapid movement of its small wings created the illusion of a small rainbow from its pink head and green and purple body. Freya smiled and watched as the hummingbird continued on its way.

"Coatlicue is a gentle soul. Are we not obligated to protect the innocent, especially those who are not warriors?" implored Abuela Monze.

"You've aged, Monze, yet you are lovely as ever. I take it this outspoken child is your kin?" said Freya pointing to Luna. Abuela Monze only nodded.

Freya addressed the group. "I am not obligated to assist you, but, I will ponder your request. In the meantime, rest and eat."

"There is no time," said Oxlac.

"Eat," ordered Freya.

Oxlac pulled out a rolled-up leaf from the pouch on his necklace. The leaf contained a pile of seeds. He began to chew them one by one and spit the shells carelessly on the forest floor. Luna reproached him with a mother's tone. "Don't you know it's rude to litter?" she said.

Oxlac motioned to the discarded shells. Luna was dumbfounded to see flowers had appeared in their place. Oxlac lifted his eyebrow, challenging Luna. "Never mind," she said, trying not to be impressed. Luna put out her hand for a seed. Oxlac obliged. She spat out the shell and expected a flower to sprout, but the discarded shell remained unchanged.

"It is rude to litter," said Oxlac without changing his calm expression. Outsmarted, Luna decided it was best to change the subject.

"Why do we need Freya's help? Out of all the gods, why her?" asked Luna.

"She has powerful magic."

"More powerful than yours?" teased Luna.

"Perhaps," replied Oxlac with a small grin.

Luna left Oxlac to his seeds. She joined her Abuela and Freya at the table with wine and fruit. Luna sniffed a few containers hoping for water, but instead inhaled what could only be the scent of wine. "I'm not old enough to drink wine," Luna told Freya. Amused, Freya took her chalice and collected water from the nearby stream. She handed it to Luna and said, "Tell me, young one, why should I help Oxlac?"

"Because only cowards turn their back on injustice," replied Luna without hesitation. She could tell the unexpected abruptness caught Freya off guard, but it did not matter. Luna always chose the possibility of punishment for the freedom to speak what was in her heart. Oxlac and Monze froze, hoping the goddess had not been offended. Freya smiled and walked into the forest and out of sight.

"Where did she go?" asked Luna. Monze and Oxlac exchanged unsure glances.

"We will wait," ordered Oxlac.

Not more than a few minutes had passed when the forest began to rumble and echo with the sound of snapping tree branches. A gigantic boar wearing gold and red armor emerged, immediately followed by a chariot led by two enormous black cats. In the chariot was Freya. She wore a helmet and bronze chest plate. The chariot stopped at Luna's feet.

"I am no coward," said Freya.

"I know," said Luna with cool confidence, pleased her words had incited the reaction she had intended.

"You will help us?" asked Abuela Monze.

"Yes," said Freya.

As if sensing her commands, the large felines pulled Freya's chariot toward the forest. "Follow me," she ordered.

~

Luna could not tell how long they had been walking. As Freya led them deeper into the forest, the trees above blocked out the sunlight and left Luna and her fellow travelers in near darkness.

48

Oxlac continued to eat from his never-ending pile of seeds, spitting out the shells over his shoulder. Luna observed with wonder as a trail of colorful flowers sprouted at his heels.

"Where are we going?" asked Luna. The knot in her stomach told her she would not like the answer.

"To retrieve my cloak," said Freya.

The massive felines pulled Freya's chariot at a slow pace so that she was only a few feet in front of Luna and the others on foot. The boar trotted behind the group, keeping a watchful eye on the ominous forest.

"Can't you just bring a different coat? Aren't we supposed to be in a hurry?" urged Luna.

"Have you forgotten my stories already?" Abuela Monze asked Luna.

"I remember Freya's necklace, but not the coat."

"Cloak, not coat," said Abuela Monze. "Her cloak is made of enchanted falcon feathers which allows the person wearing it to shape shift and travel anywhere through time and space."

"Where is the cloak?" asked Luna.

"I loaned it to someone," answered Freya.

"Loki," said Oxlac. His tone seemed to be a question and a statement at the same time. Freya looked at Oxlac and nodded yes.

Abuela Monze nervously observed the forest growing darker the deeper they roamed through the thickening trees. With every few steps the spaces between the trunks grew smaller and the floral aromas from the meadow gave way to a dank, musty stench. Abuela Monze walked with her arms wrapped protectively around Luna.

Freya observed tenderly and turned to Oxlac. "That is how the bond between your earth goddess and her daughter should be."

"Why is Coyol-what's-her-face so awful?" Luna asked of Oxlac. "Doesn't she love her mother?"

Oxlac shook his head. "The star gods do not know love. They were only taught war."

"But it's still wrong," said Luna angrily. "She shouldn't hurt her mother."

Oxlac stopped and turned to Luna. "Who do we blame, little rat? The student or the teacher? For one cannot learn what one is not taught."

As Luna stopped to absorb the meaning of Oxlac's words, she was suddenly aware the forest was permeated in a brown haze that reeked of sulfur.

"Something bad is here," said Luna as she felt one of her feelings coming on.

Freya dismounted the chariot and ordered her animal companions to return home. She raised her shield. "Get behind me," she ordered. Abuela Monze placed Luna behind Freya.

"An ogre is near," said Oxlac.

"How do you know?" asked Luna.

"They stink," said Abuela Monze to Luna.

"Try not to run. They have excellent hearing. Be as quiet as possible," ordered Freya.

Oxlac unsheathed a sizable dagger and handed it to Luna.

"Be brave, little rat," he urged.

There was a loud crack among the trees. Freya motioned for silence. "It knows we're here," Freya whispered. "Brace yourselves."

A giant ogre burst forth from the fog. Its massive feet stomped violently into the soft earth. Luna and her companions scattered in a panic to avoid being crushed. Abuela Monze and Luna hid behind the trunk of a tree. Freya raised her hands into the air and thrust them forward. As she did, hundreds of birds flew from the trees and attacked the giant's face. It swung wildly and stumbled, knocking over several trees. Oxlac ran for cover as a tree came crashing down only inches from him.

The massive ogre steadied itself and listened carefully. It swooped its arm and made a grab for Abuela Monze. Luna grabbed the dagger and stabbed the putrid-smelling ogre's hand. It yowled in pain and swung its arm angrily against the trees. The force sent Freya flying. The ogre seized the opportunity to attack the goddess and raised an angry fist. Freya's boar emerged from the trees and fog and charged the attacker. It rammed its sharp tusks into the ogre's ankle. The ogre dropped to its knees from the pain.

"Cover your ears," screamed Freya. She raised her hands. The still air suddenly whipped violently with a wild wind. As Freya brought her hands together, a small tornado formed and emitted an ear-piercing sound. The blind ogre winced in pain. Freya released the small tornado, sending it hurling towards the ogre. The ball of high-pitched winds knocked the giant on its back. It rose quickly and ran into the safety of the dark forest.

Relieved they were safe, Abuela Monze held Luna in a long embrace. Oxlac ripped a piece of material from his clothing and wiped mud from Freya's face. Freya's boar waited patiently at her feet. She knelt down and whispered to the burly creature, "Thank you, my friend. Now you must return home and wait for me." The boar obeyed and trotted off into the forest. Luna and her companions walked only a few feet when the fog cleared to reveal a lush, green clearing with a tremendous cherry blossom tree at the center. Falling flower petals created a shower of pink and white.

Freya approached the cherry blossom tree. "Come out, Loki, I know you're here."

A tall, handsome man wearing a cloak stepped from behind the large tree. He doubled over in laughter, "I've seen insects braver than you lot. All that fuss over nothing."

"That was very pernicious of you to send the giant," said Freya. "Can't you see I have guests?"

"Yes, which made it all the more amusing," he said between bursts of laughter. Loki's radiant eyes and dashing smile made it difficult to immediately dislike him, which Luna was trying her best to do. If it wasn't for his unruly demeanor, Luna would have thought he was an angel.

"Do not jest, Loki. Someone could have been hurt."

Loki pouted. "You're no fun." He patted Oxlac on the head, which the shaman did not care for, and in the most gentleman-like manner bowed to Monze and kissed her hand.

"You grow more beautiful with age, my dear Monze."

"Don't waste your efforts on me, Loki. I know you too well to be flattered."

Loki bowed deeply, a playful smile on his lips. "If you know me so well, then you know I will not give you what you came for."

"Behave Loki," said Freya.

"And what will you give me if I'm a good boy?" Loki asked flirtatiously.

"I don't have time for games today," said Freya.

Loki laughed and clapped his hands excitedly. "But I love games." He stroked the feathers of the cloak. "What do you think? It suits me, does it not?"

Freya approached Loki as he stepped back cautiously. She grabbed his arm and firmly brought him forward to kiss his cheek. "You must return my cloak," she ordered with a gentle warning.

"I don't have to do anything."

"Don't make this difficult, Loki."

"You mean difficult for you. Nothing is difficult for me."

A falling feather from Oxlac's headdress caught Luna's attention. A small pile had accumulated at his feet. Luna whispered to Oxlac. He nodded and gave his back to Freya and Loki. Freya raised her hands, preparing to call upon her magic.

"There is no time for this, Loki," she warned.

"What's the rush, my love?" said Loki, slightly intrigued.

"I owe my friend a favor," said Freya as she motioned to Oxlac, "so I must insist."

"No," said Loki. A sinister smile crawled along his face. "Having my way is much more entertaining."

Luna stepped toward Loki. "What if we play a game for it?"

Loki inspected Luna and grimaced. "What is that?"

"Little rat," Oxlac answered as he spat out a seed.

"I am not a rat. I'm a human child and I'm challenging you."

Loki burst into laughter. "Aren't you amusing!"

Oxlac handed Luna a cloak made of feathers from his headdress.

"Where did you get that?" asked Loki.

"Magic," said Luna with a smile. "If you can tell me which cloak is Freya's, then you can keep it."

"That's simple. It's the one I'm wearing. You're not very bright, child."

"I'm not finished. I will hold up both cloaks and then you must decide."

"Ha! You think I'm a fool. You'll run off with it or return it to Freya."

"I'll make everyone stand far from me. You can stay close so there is no way I can run away or give the cloak to Freya. I bet you wouldn't be able to tell which is which. I hear you're not very bright."

Loki gasped, slightly pained by the insult. "Don't let my ravishing good looks fool you. I am as clever as they come." He laughed with the fervor of a mischievous child. "You think you can outwit me. I am so curious as to how you plan to trick me. For that reason alone, I accept your challenge."

"Everyone, except Loki, take one hundred steps back," ordered Luna.

"Absolutely not," said Abuela Monze. "He can hurt you."

"Please, Abuela. I know what I'm doing."

Oxlac gave Abuela Monze a reassuring nod. She backed away, and with hesitation joined Freya and Oxlac who had already taken one hundred steps back. Loki giggled and readied himself to outsmart Luna. He handed her Freya's cloak. Luna held up both feather-covered cloaks.

"Okay, Loki. Is it this cloak?" Luna asked, as she held up Oxlac's faux cloak. "Or is it this one?"

As Luna held up Freya's cloak, she quickly released it and let it drape over her. Oxlac's cloak fell to the ground as Luna transformed herself into a small yellow bird and took to the sky.

"You wicked child!" screamed Loki. He turned to Freya.

"Fair is fair," she said as she blew him a kiss.

The small yellow bird flew into Freya's open hand and transformed into Luna. Still dizzy from her first shape-shifting experience, Luna did not notice as Freya swiftly wrapped herself and her companions with the cloak of falcon feathers. To Loki's dismay, they disappeared instantly before his eyes.

CHAPTER 5

THE POET

The Poet had not left his home since his night with Coatlicue. A storm of thoughts and emotions kept his logical mind at bay. Preferring solitude in the darkness of confusion and disappointment, he lay for days in his bed. Even his writing utensils sat untouched. Rolls of parchment sat discarded and blank, naked of their customary poetry. Time passed in unknown increments as The Poet lay in bed and stared at a single white feather on a small table, a keepsake from Coatlicue's bedroom. He felt as though his mind and heart were no longer his. He struggled between fits of sadness and rage at his mind's unrelenting attachment to the goddess. He wanted nothing more than to fall apart in her arms again, but also at the same time, forget her completely. He replayed each moment with Coatlicue over and over. A ceaseless flow of memories attacked him. In sporadic moments of clarity, The Poet would pray his heartache would not devour him. To the relief of his soul, he would fall into short slumbers and his mind rested temporarily.

Obligation finally lured The Poet out of his melancholy state. On the fifth day of his heart's mourning, he received a letter politely demanding his presence at the king's palace. His fellow architects were gathering to discuss plans to expand the floating gardens, which would require The Poet's superior math skills.

Disobedience was a severely punishable offense, but it was the prospect of being rude that motivated The Poet to instruct his servants to prepare him for a proper outing. One servant poured water over hot stones for his bath, while another laid out his clothing. As his thoughts drifted, The Poet stepped into the round stone tub and bathed slowly. He dressed in a cotton tunic decorated with colorful embroidery and feathers. After breakfast, a servant handed The Poet an ornately carved fan covered with an array of beautiful, large feathers, a status symbol he was in no mood to carry about.

The Poet stepped outside and paused a few moments to absorb the warmth of the sun. He took his time walking along the stone paved pathways. He passed the white washed clay homes of the upper class. The hissing of water over hot stones filled the air as servants prepared their masters' baths. As he passed the homes of the middle and lower classes, similar sounds filled the air, sizzling steam from freshly poured baths and families sitting down to breakfast. Parents rushed past The Poet with a "Good morning" as they hurried their children to school. Education was a requirement, regardless of social status.

As The Poet neared the tree line into the jungle, he saw the Wise Woman's hut. He hoped her renowned powers of healing and wisdom could cure him. She stood in the doorway with a warm and welcoming smile. The Wise Woman was small in stature. Jet black hair with streaks of white lay smoothly down her back. Despite her elevated rank, she insisted on living near the poor and preferred simple earth-colored garments. The smell of incense and flower water emitted from the open door as The Poet drew near.

"Please forgive the intrusion," he said.

"You are always welcome in my home," she said, and guided The Poet to sit with her.

"So, tell me why you are here," she said.

The Poet began to speak. The Wise Woman silenced him. "I already know what troubles you. What do you want of me?"

The Poet could not find his words. He sat in silence ashamed of his suffering.

"Consider your pain a gift. Not many poets truly know the elation and agony of love," said the Wise Woman, who possessed the gift of *sight*.

"I cannot bear this. Please heal me. Take this from me," said The Poet.

"I will tell you what to do."

"You can heal me?"

The Wise Woman shook her head. "There is nothing I can do for you," she said and smiled.

"If I cannot be healed, why do you smile?"

"You will see," she said tenderly.

"You will leave me to suffer, then?"

"Patience."

"Patience?" The Poet asked.

"Yes. Have patience. Now you must leave."

"Is there no cleansing to be done?"

The Wise Woman picked up a bushel of herbs sitting among her shelves of remedies and smacked The Poet roughly with them. He shielded himself from the unexpected flurry.

"Now go," she said, and embraced him.

"Thank you. We will meet again soon," he said.

"Goodbye, Poet," said the Wise Woman, knowing they would never meet again. She smiled to herself as her guest went on his way, amused by what she had foreseen in The Poet's near future.

The Poet proceeded toward the city center. He passed various waterways and fountains that flowed throughout the entire kingdom carrying fresh water to the rich and poor. Colorful flowers dangled from lush green plants that lined the waterways and gardens. He arrived at the busy market place and made his way through the crowds. The flowing movement of hundreds of merchants and patrons were like waves in an uneasy ocean. Cries from the animals awaiting sale and shouts from the eager vendors filled the humid air.

The Poet walked slowly as he passed the floating gardens of corn, tomato, and vanilla that lined the pathways to the royal temples. The surrounding beauty slightly eased his mental disarray. The kingdom was truly a living, breathing paradise. The largest temple was surrounded by four smaller ones, all of which were adorned with murals of gods, royalty, and scenes from everyday life in rich earth tones and bright pastels. The Poet climbed the stairs of one of the smaller temples and greeted his fellow architects, who were engaged in a fervent debate over equations and measurements of the new floating gardens. The Poet sat quietly, pretending to listen. One of the senior architects took notice of his uncommon reserve.

"The greatest poet and architect in this kingdom should not look so defeated," said the old man. "What is her name? Only a woman can do this. Or a man, depending on one's preference."

"What does it matter?" said The Poet, "she hides herself from me."

The old man leaned in close to The Poet. "A word of advice, my friend?" asked the old man in a pleasant but firm tone. The Poet nodded his head with consent.

"Return to where you found her. Speak words only your magnificent mind has the power to speak, and you will move her heart. She will return to you."

"You would not instruct me to forget her?" asked The Poet.

"What kind of a poet would so readily abandon the pursuit of his heart's desire?" asked the old man.

His question was the answer to the peace The Poet was seeking. *What if she has been calling to me and I have not been listening,* The Poet thought, realizing Coatlicue had been calling out to the universe, searching for him. The Poet waited anxiously for dusk. He knew the setting sun would force the group to adjourn their gathering for the day. The Poet left the meeting as twilight fell softly over the land. He paused at a balcony to admire the star filled sky illuminating the royal temples with a magical glow.

The Poet returned to the jungle and vowed not to leave until Coatlicue returned. He stood where the staircase would have been and said quietly to himself:

My heart is heavy with love for you.

Return to me, Coatlicue

Make me whole once more.

Only your touch can stop the atrophy of my soul.

Without you nights are empty,

and so am I.

CHAPTER 6

ATHENA

Freya lifted her cloak and was relieved to see all of her companions. "I've never used the cloak with more than one person. I am pleased everyone survived the journey. However, I will have a very ill-tempered Loki to deal with upon my return," she said. Abuela Monze and Oxlac gave Freya a sympathetic nod.

Brimming with excitement, Luna leapt into the air. "Woo hoo!" she yelled, "did you see me? I did it, I shape shifted!"

"You are clever, little rat," said Oxlac sincerely.

"We have to celebrate, Oxlac. Ready? Woo hoo!" she shouted.

"Woo hoo," said Oxlac genuinely, but lacking enthusiasm.

"We are definitely going to work on that," said Luna.

Luna noticed Freya's eyes glazed with amazement. "This rivals the beauty of my land," she said. Luna turned to see they were standing on a hilltop that overlooked rolling green hills that stood out beautifully against the bright blue sky. The hills surrounded a quiet bay of crystal clear water. Lone trees stood here and there, their branches swaying gently from the constant ocean breeze. There was not a creature in sight.

"This can't be real," said Luna.

"It's always a sight to see," said Abuela Monze in a soft tone that warmed Luna's heart. The familiarity of her abuela's voice comforted Luna and the tension and fear momentarily slipped from her body. The serenity of the landscape was so tempting that Luna and her companions could not help but pause and relish their surroundings. Abuela Monze sat in the soft green grass, grateful for a moment's rest. Oxlac opened the small pouch he wore dangling around his neck and began sifting through the contents. The pouch was only the size of an apple, but somehow his entire hand fit inside as if the small bag was bottomless. Freya invited Luna to sit with her in the soft grass.

"Oxlac must be fond of you," Freya said to Luna.

"Me? "Why do you think that?"

"He called you a rat. He adores rodents. He believes them to be quite resourceful."

Luna was pleased. For as odd as he was, she admired the shaman. Freya lay back and rested her head against the earth; her golden red hair spread out and contrasted vibrantly against the green grass and small, colorful flowers. Luna followed Freya's example and reclined in the soft pasture. She had not realized how damp and cold she was from the forest until she felt goosebumps rising on her skin from the sun's warmth. She also realized she was tired and hungry. Luna tried to distract her thoughts from food. She imagined what the goddess Athena would be like. Abuela Monze had always described Athena as a fearsome warrior in her stories. Luna hoped she would not be unpleasant. Still aware of the ache in her belly, Luna looked around for another distraction and noticed her Abuela meditating with her back to the group.

Luna whispered to Freya, "If all of you are so powerful, why do you need my grandmother?"

"Because she is a healer, which makes her very important. And you, I see, are not without your talents."

"Me?" asked Luna

"I would not have been prepared for the ogre if you had not sensed it so quickly," said Freya. Luna smiled for the first time since their journey began. She had always loved hearing stories of Freya and so a compliment from her was enough to distract Luna from their precarious circumstances. Luna closed her eyes and took in more of the warm sun. There was a peaceful silence over the group until Oxlac began to grumble with impatience as he continued to search through his pouch.

"What are you looking for?" asked Abuela Monze.

"My shell. Oxlac must call Athena," he said.

"Can't you just change into a bird and fly to her?" asked Luna.

"Oxlac cannot leave you. It is not safe," he said as he pulled out a tiny shell from the pouch. He rubbed it between his hands and blew on it hard, as if trying to remove dust. The shell grew instantly to the size of a large conch. Oxlac took a deep breath, but before he could blow into the shell, Luna was suddenly overwhelmed with dread. She sat up and involuntarily yelled, "Get down!" Freya swiftly yanked Luna back down into the grass.

Before Abuela Monze could realize what was happening, Oxlac had already dove to the ground and knocked Monze on her back. Deafening screeching filled the air. Luna opened her eyes just as a swarm of flying creatures flew inches from Luna and the others. The creatures grabbed at them with razor-sharp talons, only missing the group by inches. Luna shielded her head as she felt the creatures whoosh by inches from her face, causing the air to hit her with unexpected force. The creatures screeched louder, infuriated to have missed their targets.

Abuela Monze looked up to see dozens of flying hybrid creatures the size of elephants, each with the body of a lion and the head of an eagle. She watched one of the hybrid beasts dive intently toward Luna. Before Abuela Monze could shout a warning, Freya flung herself between Luna and the beast. The goddess screamed in pain as the creature's claws ripped through her flesh, digging deep into her shoulders. The creature rose abruptly and lifted Freya into the air. Several creatures bit and snatched at Freya as she dangled, exposed, but not helpless. In an instant, she summoned her magic and the surrounding beasts dropped to the ground as they were hit by an invisible force. A wave of winged creatures appeared and quickly outnumbered Freya.

As the beast flapped its veiny wings to take flight with Freya, Luna jumped and grabbed her by the leg. Luna pulled out the knife Oxlac had given her and began stabbing wildly as the flying creatures tried to attack her. Oxlac and Monze rushed to their aid, but were immediately overwhelmed with a vicious onslaught. Oxlac knelt and reached frantically into his pouch. He pulled out an ax-like weapon and began swinging at the creatures with fierce precision.

"Find the shell. You must call Athena," he shouted to Abuela Monze.

Luna clung to Freya's leg and pulled with all her might as Abuela Monze crawled along the ground looking for the conch shell. Two more flying beasts attempted to snatch Freya away, but only managed to rip off her cloak. Their angry screeches rose to an unbearable pitch as they flew away, still fighting over the cloak.

Freya's captor held tight. She screamed again as the creature's serrated claws tore deeper into her flesh. Her arms now dangled uselessly at her sides. Blood gushed from the long, deep wounds.

Luna watched helplessly as Freya struggled to call her magic. The goddess closed her eyes and inhaled deeply to concentrate, but too much blood had left her body and she lost consciousness.

A glimmer of pink among the green grass caught Abuela Monze's attention. She shielded her head and ran toward the shell. Talons and callused wings made for a difficult path. Monze was knocked to the ground, but reached out and took hold of the shell. She took in a rapid, deep breath and blew into the shell. The sound boomed across the rolling green hills toward Mount Olympus.

The goddess Athena stood quietly, in deep contemplation, as she read from the pages of an ancient manuscript in the great library. The only sound was a sharp hiss that would break the silence each time she turned a page. Thousands of books and scrolls filled ornately carved shelves. Gold statues and delicately painted vases and portraits adorned the tables and walls.

The call of Oxlac's shell snapped Athena out of her concentration. Knowing there could only be one reason for the familiar sound, she hastened across the palace of the gods until she reached her personal armory. Athena emerged in full armor, her spear in one hand and a goat skin shield in the other. An impressive sword was strapped to her back.

Athena heard a voice from behind her sternly ask, "Where are you going?" Athena turned to face the god Zeus. His formidable figure towered over hers.

"To assist a friend," replied Athena calmly.

"I cannot guarantee your safety if you leave this mountain."

"I know," said Athena with a smile.

As she bounded down the stairs of Mount Olympus, a white owl swooped down and landed on her shoulders. A gray horse awaited her at the bottom of the marble steps. Athena heard the call of Oxlac's shell once more. Without haste, she mounted the stallion and charged toward the distress call, holding tight to the stallion's mane as they rode at full speed.

Athena could hear the chaos as her mare approached the hills near the sea. Soon the flying creatures came into view. Her white owl took flight and landed in a nearby tree for safety. Athena squeezed her legs tightly to hold onto to the stallion as she unsheathed her weapons, her sword in one hand and the spear in the other. Without hesitation, she charged into the madness and cut down several creatures at once. They continued to fall dead or fly away as Athena attacked with ferocity.

"Come on, then," she screamed as she wielded her sword.

Luna had never seen such a sight. It was like watching a giant swatting butterflies, not because of Athena's size, but because of her brutish strength and accuracy. Athena moved so swiftly Luna could hardly keep track of her movements. The beasts fell from the sky like rain. Blood flew everywhere as Athena made her way towards Freya's dangling body. Luna still held tightly to Freya's legs to keep the rabid beast from flying away with her. Taking only a moment to aim, Athena threw her spear and took down Freya's captor. The creature dropped the goddess and spiraled to the ground. Oxlac jumped to catch Freya and barely stopped her from crashing into the hard earth.

In no time all, the assailing creatures were dead or had flown away in fear. Luna and the others were about to breathe sighs of relief when Athena abruptly shouted, "Look!" The group braced themselves for the worst, but only a hummingbird flew near and stopped to drink the nectar from a large yellow flower. Athena turned to the group, her long black hair and angular face covered in blood. Her large, dark eyes widened. "Aren't they beautiful," she said ardently. Luna's heart pounded in her chest from adrenaline. She nodded in agreement purely out of a polite reflex, her head still spinning from their near-death experience.

Several familiar figures swooped down and landed in the surrounding trees. Athena looked up at the winged creatures and said, "Anyone else care to play?" They shifted on the branches with hesitation and wrapped their leathery wings around their bodies as a sign of submission. Satisfied, Athena took Oxlac's hand in hers.

"My old friend, how good it is to see you," Athena said to the shaman. Luna was surprised by the warmth in Athena's voice.

Athena turned and observed the wounds on Freya's back. She addressed Oxlac and Abuela Monze directly: "Freya is most beloved. Pray you won't have to answer to Odin for these injuries. Dare I ask what peril has lured you away from the safety of your homelands? And speak quickly. The inhabitants here do not like strangers."

"You must leave with us," said the fatigued shaman.

Athena turned to Oxlac and said, "Although I enjoy your company, the reasons behind your visits are never pleasant."

"We need your protection," said Abuela Monze. "A life must be saved, and I'm afraid bloodshed will be required to accomplish this."

"And whose life must I save?" asked Athena as she wiped her sword clean with the bottom of her leather skirt. Luna cringed at the sight of more blood.

"Coatlicue's," said Oxlac.

"Your earth goddess? She's harmless. Who could have quarrel with such a gentle creation?"

"She will be punished with death," said Oxlac.

"For what?"

"The father of her child is a mortal man."

"That is no crime," scoffed Athena.

"It is in my land."

"She cannot defend herself," said Athena.

"That is why we are here," interjected Abuela Monze.

Athena glanced at Luna. "The child weakens you. Why did you bring her?" she asked.

"We had no choice," said Monze.

"Well, then, I will join you," said Athena.

"That's it? You're not going to make us beg you or answer a riddle," asked Luna incredulously.

"What a waste of time that would be," said Athena.

"Is this a trick? Why are you making this so easy?" asked Luna skeptically.

"Because I hate injustice," Athena said sternly. Then, with a playful smile on her lips she added, "And I love to fight."

Athena mounted her horse. "Prepare yourselves for the wrath of my land," she said.

Luna whispered to her abuela, "What does she mean by wrath? Weren't all of those monsters enough wrath?" Abuela Monze touched Luna lightly on the shoulder, her silent command for composure, and remained kneeling and held tightly to Freya.

"Freya must rest," said Monze to Athena.

"She can't die, right?" asked Luna.

"Only a god can kill a god, child, but we can be injured," said Athena. "Very well," she continued, "we must make our way to Mount Olympus. It is the only safe place here."

Oxlac lifted Freya and cradled her carefully. He turned to Luna. "Do not fret, little rat. She will heal," he said.

"Here, put her on my horse," ordered Athena.

"No need," said Oxlac as he carried Freya.

"You are very polite, Oxlac. I really like that," said Luna and she meant it. She thought to herself how her mother would approve of Oxlac's chivalry. Luna realized she hadn't thought of her mother until that moment, and hoped she was still sound asleep.

"Oxlac must be kind. He must respect," said Oxlac.

"Scaring my poor son-in-law was not good manners, Oxlac," said Abuela Monze reproachfully. The shaman tried to hide his amusement.

Luna looked Oxlac in the eye and squinted with authority. "Hey, you better be nice to my dad," she ordered. Her regard for Oxlac slipped slightly into a momentary pool of dislike.

Oxlac nodded humbly and said, "I promise to be polite."

Luna and the others followed behind Athena. They walked with guarded steps and kept a careful eye on their surroundings. Only the occasional cry of an unseen bird broke their silence. They did not get far before Luna felt a pang of anxiety.

"I'm scared," she said to her abuela.

"Just keep walking," said Abuela Monze as she looked cautiously over her shoulder.

Several feet away from the group sat the opening of a cave on a rocky hillside. The shadow of the cavern entrance sent a pang of fear through Luna. The generous bunches of flowers which had sprouted at the foot of the opening did little to disguise the menacing impression.

"Something bad is in there," Luna said with a shaky voice.

Athena dismounted her horse and motioned for the group to remain still. She raised her shield and sword as she approached the cave. Luna observed her with admiration. Athena was truly a formidable sight. A low, angry growl met Athena as she drew near the cave's dark entrance. Luna could not believe something could be more terrifying than the flying demons, but there it was. A goat's head sat unnaturally on the shoulders of a lion's body. In place of a tail was a long, ugly snake that hissed and snapped at the air. Luna wanted to run, but her body felt disconnected from the promptings of her brain, so she remained frozen in fear. *Well, at least it can't really hurt us. Goats don't have sharp teeth*, she thought to herself, but then the animal rose on its hind legs and roared. A burst of flames shot out of its mouth.

"Never mind," Luna whispered to herself.

The goat-headed beast sprinted past Athena and headed straight toward Freya's bleeding body, its grotesque mouth ready for attack. Oxlac was only left with a moment to embrace Freya so she would not be burned. "Oxlac," called Athena as she flung her shield through the air. Oxlac raised the shield in time to block the scorching flames.

Athena threw her spear, but missed her mark as the beast zigzagged with precision to avoid the deadly weapon. Without stopping, it bolted after Luna. She never imagined she would be terrified of a goat. Abuela Monze wrapped herself protectively around Luna. Athena charged at the beast, despite knowing she would not reach it before the flames hit Monze and Luna.

Petrified of being burned to death, Luna closed her eyes. She could hear the crackling of the blaze, but felt no heat. She looked up and saw the flames stopped in mid-air, as if hitting a wall of glass. Luna looked over to see Freya with half-opened eyes, concentrating on the space blocking the flames.

~

Zeus stepped out to an empty courtyard with a round, marble fountain overflowing with wine. A maze of rose bushes and fruit trees surrounded the courtyard. "Show me Athena," Zeus said to the fountain. The moving images of Luna and the others projected on the liquid surface. Zeus observed the assault with no reaction.

"She could use some assistance with the chimera," said a nearby voice. "Battle is most difficult when there are others to protect than just oneself," the voice urged.

"I told her not to leave," said Zeus.

"They have a human child with them. She could be killed."

"I don't have time for this," Zeus huffed as he thrust his arm toward the sky, sending a lightning bolt into the clear blue. A loud clap of thunder cracked through the air, and dark clouds spread across the sky like spilt ink.

"Don't expect me to do anything else," Zeus said.

A centaur in full armor stepped forward and bowed graciously.

"Since you are so concerned, you will escort them, Chiron" ordered Zeus as he walked away. The centaur bowed obediently.

~

Dark clouds rolled overhead and a drenching rain was upon them. Athena leaped into the air and drove her sword into the chimera's back with a mighty thrust. The hybrid beast roared in pain and reared itself, but the rainstorm squelched the combustion before it could leave its throat. Oxlac stood shielding the others, clutching tightly to his medicine bag, prepared to use the last of his magic if necessary. Athena circled the chimera, ready to strike, but the beast lowered itself in submission as the sheets of rain extinguished its fiery breath. Finally defeated, the chimera retreated to its cave.

Luna and Abuela Monze huddled closely and did their best to shelter Freya from the torrent. Luna's heart sank as she made out several figures approaching in the distance. It would be impossible to stave off another attack without Freya. To Luna's relief, the figures were humans riding horses. As Athena took a moment to catch her breath, she noticed the quickly-approaching figures through the sheets of downpour. As they drew near, the rain subsided.

"I could have managed, Chiron," said Athena.

"Zeus' orders," replied Chiron calmly.

"I have no doubt you had a hand in persuading him," said Athena sarcastically, but with affection.

Chiron smiled and bowed.

Luna had spent the short duration of the greeting gawking at the group of centaurs. Their bodies were formed in such a way to appear as if a human man had been cut in half and a horse's legs and back had been attached where the pelvic area and legs should have been. Their naked torsos were slick from the rain, which had now ceased. Metal helmets covered most of their faces, but left enough of their features in view for Luna to see they did not appear entirely human. They had pointed features she imagined a gnome or a fairy would have.

"He's a horse," blurted Luna.

"He is a centaur," corrected Athena.

"Shall we?" invited Chiron. Athena mounted her horse. One of the accompanying centaurs kneeled to allow Abuela Monze onto his back. Another centaur approached Luna and kneeled. She backed away.

"You will be safe," said Athena to Luna.

Luna mounted the centaur's back and was unsure where to grasp, since there was no saddle or reins. As the centaur took his first steps, Luna wobbled and quickly decided his waist would have to do. Oxlac lifted Freya onto Athena's horse. Athena wrapped her arm about Freya's waist and pulled on the reins, prompting her stallion into a steady gallop. Luna made sure to keep her eye on Oxlac. It would have been amusing to see the shaman riding a centaur, but to Luna's disappointment, Oxlac opted to shape-shift into a goldfinch and fly to Mount Olympus.

The sun had re-appeared and cast down a welcomed heat upon the group of shivering, wet bodies. Athena and the centaurs galloped at lightning speed. If there were other monsters in their path, Luna and the others would not have known; the group rode too fast through the valley to be seen or bothered with. Luna was relieved when she felt her centaur slow to a trot and slowly ascend stairs which led to the entrance of an enormous white temple-like structure. They were greeted by a dozen female servants who immediately led them to an inner room with natural hot spring baths and marble tables filled with various fruits and meats. The room was lit by candles and decorated with countless flowers and exquisite pottery.

The servants stationed themselves at the foot of each bathing pool with piles of material in various pastel hues folded in their arms. Luna could only assume the materials were to be their towels. The servants were shorter than Luna, yet looked like grown women. They had long, curly hair of various colors, and pointed ears. Too famished and exhausted for modesty, Luna quickly disrobed and sat in a bath eating handfuls of grapes and cheese. Freya jolted to life as she was placed into a small pool of gently bubbling water. Servants poured cool water over the wounds on her back. After only a few minutes, Luna watched as Freya was assisted from the water by three of the servant women and led out of sight. A freshly-bathed Abuela Monze followed closely behind Freya.

"Where are they going? Why did they leave?" Luna asked Athena, now too worried to enjoy her much-needed bath.

"Relax, little rat," said Athena without opening her eyes and interrupting the comfort of the hot, soothing water.

After what felt like an hour, Luna was tapped on the shoulder and gently guided to exit to another room, where she and Athena were dried off and dressed. Luna looked down at the long gown she'd been given and gasped. The silk was a soft shade of lavender with shiny gold seams. The material wrapped around her perfectly and made a swishing motion as she walked. Athena, however, wore the same type of plain, brown leather top and skirt. "I don't do silk," she said to Luna.

Luna and Athena were led to another room filled with extravagant sofas and armchairs. The smell of eucalyptus saturated the air in the room. Luna recognized Abuela Monze's figure in the

79

candlelit room. Monze delicately wrapped gauze around Freya's wounds; she whispered and hummed as Freya slept soundly. Oxlac sat warming himself near a fire. His headdress sat on a footstool and Luna realized she had not yet seen the shaman without his feathery adornment. Oxlac motioned for silence as Luna took a seat near him. She noticed his body paint was perfectly intact, though his long, black hair appeared damp.

"Did you take a bath?" asked Luna.

"Bathing is very important to my people."

"So I guess that means yes," said Luna, between confusion and sarcasm. How the shaman could bathe and repaint his entire body in so little time was a mystery Luna was too tired to uncover, so she settled quietly next to Oxlac. The heat from the fire sent waves of goosebumps across her skin. Just as she drifted into a delicious sleep, the doors burst open. Zeus entered the room and addressed Athena without looking at the others.

"You know I don't care for uninvited guests," he snapped.

"It was necessary," replied Athena coolly.

Oxlac rose from his seat near the fire and stepped forward. Zeus softened at the familiar face. "Forgive my temper old friend, you are always welcome," said Zeus.

Oxlac bowed his head in greeting.

"Whatever you need, it will be done," said Zeus.

"Take us to Hades."

"That I will not do."

"You must," replied Oxlac sternly.

"Are you mad? He would kill you all," replied Zeus, his temper rising.

"We need passage through the underworld to see Isis," said Athena.

"That cannot be done. You should know better," said Zeus.

"Please. If you don't help, Coatlicue will die," said Luna.

"Really? A damsel in distress. Can we think of nothing new? Better keep quiet, child. Your presence here has already caused me an ill dose of discontent," said Zeus as he waved his great arms about, openly displaying his annoyance.

"Why won't you help us?" asked Luna, the embers of her temper sparked by the god's sarcasm.

"I would assist, but Hades and I are not on the best of terms," said Zeus.

"Well, duh," said Luna, "but you're Zeus. Aren't you the ruler here?"

"I cannot control the actions of others, only punish them if I see fit. Hades is merciless. You would not survive."

"I must ask you do this for me," Athena said sternly. "We cannot refuse Oxlac. You are very well aware he has aided us on more than one occasion."

Zeus thought a few moments and finally gestured toward Abuela Monze. "If you brought her, then it must be grave," he said to Oxlac. "You have been a useful ally, shaman, and for that reason only I will escort you to Hades, but I will not intervene on your behalf. And I cannot guarantee your interaction will be pleasant. Think carefully. Are you sure of this request?"

"No choice," said Oxlac, "it must be done."

"Then follow me," said Zeus.

Zeus led them down a corridor which ended at a metal door that reached to the ceiling. Freya walked slowly, with Oxlac's assistance. Zeus grabbed the handle and braced himself as he pried open the heavy door. Luna and the others were met with an overpowering stench; even the mighty Zeus turned away in disgust.

"Always impossible to bear," he grimaced.

A cage with wooden bars dangled by a thick rope over a pit in the earth. Zeus unhinged the door and held it open. A wooden plank of questionable stability was the only path over the pit and onto the cage-like elevator.

"I'm not going in there," said Luna as she held tightly to her abuela. "I want to go home," she whimpered.

"This is our only way home, mija," said Abuela Monze. The soothing confidence in her voice was just enough to coax Luna forward. Oxlac and Freya stepped carefully onto the rickety elevator. Oxlac reached out his hands to Luna and Monze as they balanced each step onto their precarious transportation. Athena stepped aboard without hesitation. Zeus handed Athena a torch and hissed, "Return here alive, Athena, or so help me."

Zeus loosened the rope and slowly lowered the elevator by hand. "Close your eyes until you feel you've hit the bottom of the cavern," he said to Luna.

Luna opened her eyes and immediately regretted her decision. The flames from the torch bounced off the walls with a frantic light intensifying the frightening surroundings. Luna realized there were human bones sticking out of the wall, stacked in groups, like bricks in a building. White bony fingers and the black eye sockets of skulls jumped out from the darkness each time the torch neared the macabre structure. The pungent stench worsened the further they descended. Luna squeezed her eyes shut until they reached the bottom and hit the stone floor with a jarring thud. The elevator began rising back up as soon as they dismounted the cage. Luna opened her eyes to complete darkness, save for the dwindling light from the torch which only illuminated Athena's face. The goddess of war held out the torch and turned from side to side as she decided which way they should proceed.

"How dare you enter this place!" boomed a deep voice from behind them, which startled even Oxlac.

Athena held up the torch in the voice's direction. "We only ask passage to the underworld of Isis," said Athena with a hint of hesitation.

"There is only death down here," said the voice with a vile growl that made Luna shutter.

"Who is that?" Luna whispered to her abuela.

"Hades," answered Monze in a cautious whisper.

"If you allow us passage, there will be no quarrel," said Athena. "I give you my word. And you will be compensated well for your cooperation."

"Compensated," Hades repeated with a menacing laugh. "What have I to want for in this haven?" he asked facetiously.

"Let us pass, Hades, or you will have Zeus to answer to," warned Athena.

"Your father is not here now, is he? So, I think, you are at my mercy."

"I do not fear you, old man," said Athena as she tightened her grip on the fading torch.

A towering figure stepped toward the flame and a hideous, twisted face came into view. Luna had never been so terrified in her life; she understood what it meant to be frozen in fear. She imagined the same trepidation would be felt by a camper unexpectedly facing a bear. One by one, the extinguished torches hanging from long dead skeletons, began to light aflame along the walls of the dank cave.

Luna looked around and saw they were in a small chamber surrounded by several closed doors. A black slimy substance dripped down the walls and the room was filled with a putrid smell that reminded Luna the time her father had discovered a dead opossum was rotting under their house.

"I will not assist you," he sneered with black, sharp teeth and twisted his face in a most unsightly expression. "Though I might keep you here as my slaves, especially the human child. I will feed her to my hounds and use whatever remains to rot and feed the maggots in this rotten earth."

Luna stuck out her tongue and crossed her arms to stop herself from shaking. She did her best not to run and hide behind her Abuela. Luna would have preferred the fire breathing goat over Hades. The other creatures they'd encountered had been dangerous, but they were brainless, acting out of their animalistic impulses, save Loki, who was more mischievous than harmful. But, when Luna looked into the eyes of Hades, she could see in him a malicious soul, and for the first time in their journey she realized they might never return home.

Just as Hades took a step toward Luna, Freya gathered every ounce of strength she had and knocked Hades to his knees with her magic.

"You will pay dearly for that, wench," he seethed. "How dare you attack me here!"

Hades rose and charged Freya, but was again knocked to the ground. The sound of rocks breaking apart echoed in the cave. Abuela Monze wrapped her arms around Luna in fear of tumbling rubble. Hades was knocked to his back and began to sink into the ground. "I don't like to be called wench," said Freya angrily.

The more she clenched her fist, the lower Hades sank into the ground. Hades erupted in anger and broke free. He stood ready to decimate his enemies.

"Hades," said a petite, young woman with long, dark hair that framed her angelic face. "Please do not be unkind to our guests," she said. She approached Hades, and his fury immediately melted away as she gently touched his face.

"Allow them passage and for your unpleasant behavior, you will gift the daughter of Zeus your helmet," said Persephone sweetly.

"I will do no such thing," growled Hades.

"If you grant my wish, I will remain with you one additional month this year."

"Your mother will not allow it."

"She will understand," said Persephone.

Hades obeyed like a reluctant child. Although Persephone was his captive, she ruled him body and soul, for the god of the underworld loved her beyond his control. Hades disappeared through one of the many doors. He reappeared shortly with a glowing, golden helmet. He threw it hard at Athena. She caught it easily with one hand.

Luna was beside herself with bewilderment. She stood speechless and wondered if perhaps the mysterious woman had a spell over Hades. *How could someone hold so much power over such an evil, angry god?* Luna thought. As if Abuela Monze could read her mind, she said to Luna, "Everyone has their weakness."

Hades threw open one of the doors and made an angry exit through another. The graceful young woman followed calmly behind him.

"Persephone," called Athena. The woman turned and smiled.

"Thank you," said Athena with heartfelt gratitude.

"You are most welcome, daughter of Zeus," Persephone said, and turned to leave.

"Who is that?" Luna asked Freya.

"The reluctant queen of Hades."

"Why is she reluctant?" asked Luna, confused and surprised someone like Hades had a wife.

"She is his prisoner for half of every year. I will tell you all about her when we return home," said Abuela Monze.

Luna and the others approached the door Hades had left open. Oxlac kissed Freya's hand with over-exaggerated decorum as he guided her through the doorway. He did the same to Monze and Athena. Oxlac then extended his arm to Luna with his best gentleman-like effort. Luna accepted the invitation. She closely observed the vivid pigments on his arm. She was thoroughly puzzled the colors never dried or flaked. Luna tried to rub the paint from his arm, but it remained intact.

"You need soap," said Oxlac, which caused Luna to smile, lightening the heavy mood.

"You were brave, little rat," he continued.

"He scared me."

"But you did not show it. Warriors never show fear," said Oxlac, and stuck out his tongue to imitate Luna. Her laugh echoed among the stone walls as they descended the long, dark stairway.

CHAPTER 7

ISIS

The staircase came to a sudden end at a stone wall. The fading light from the torch only revealed shadowed glimpses of what looked to be Egyptian hieroglyphs. Freya blew gently on the dimming flame. Luna watched in awe as the fire returned to its initial luminosity. Athena held up the torch to reveal the shape of a gigantic scarab beetle that was carved in the center of the wall. Luna had been obsessed with Egyptian hieroglyphs from the very first time her abuela taught her Egyptian mythology. Unable to help herself, Luna ran her fingers along the familiar carvings. Delicate grains fell away at her touch.

"We are here," said Oxlac.

"How do we open the door?" asked Luna.

Oxlac closed his eyes and reached out to touch the wall. He took a deep breath. As he exhaled, he pushed his hand into the wall. The structure gave away like falling sand and crumbled around them. Everyone shielded their faces until the sound of rushing sand subsided. Abuela Monze and Oxlac stepped forward as if they'd already beheld the spectacle which had left the others dumbfounded. The sounds from the land registered in Luna's brain before the images of the majestic splendor. She could hear the soothing water from the immense river that lay before them. Loud calls from birds seemed to come from every direction.

Wild splashes from hunting crocodiles drew Luna's attention to the river. The heads of several crocodiles sat motionless on the water's surface. Their black, stalking eyes sent warning pangs of fear through Luna; she knew better than to enter their territory. Luna was startled by a small group of cranes that took flight as a sneaking crocodile snapped at a passing fish. She could not believe the various plants and animals that flourished about the river, despite the surrounding desert land.

The shell of a turtle floated past and stopped near the shore. It emerged slowly and disappeared into the tall, wispy grass that bordered the river. Luna turned to see an ibis as it stepped delicately through the grass and made its way toward the river's edge. She was in reverence of the beauty of its white feathers and black neck. The elegance of the ibis would be forever imprinted in her memory. Birds held a special place in Luna's heart. She had always wanted one as a pet, but thought it too cruel to keep one in a cage.

"Is that the Nile River?" asked Luna, bubbling with excitement.

"Yes, my love," said Abuela Monze.

"I've always wanted to visit Egypt," said Luna, struggling to keep her voice down. She had finally caught on to the importance of quiet entrances to new lands.

"It's beautiful, but dangerous," said Monze.

"There it is," said Oxlac, pointing to a long canoe hidden among the bamboo reeds of the river bank.

"It cannot be this easy," said Athena.

"It is not," replied Abuela Monze.

"I assume if we approach the vessel, we will be attacked," said Freya. Her strength was now fully restored. Luna noticed Freya's skin and hair glowed with the original luster of their first encounter.

"Can't we just walk?" sighed Luna. "I'd really prefer not to fight anymore monsters."

"Only the river can take us to Isis," said Abuela Monze.

A gazelle stopped near Luna to graze on the tall, willowy grass. She could not have imagined being so close to such a stunning and wild creature. Luna held her breath, afraid she would frighten the gazelle away.

"It cannot see you," said Oxlac, and smiled with amusement at Luna's curiosity.

"What do you mean it can't see me?"

"We are here, but not."

"We're invisible?" asked Luna.

"It cannot see through the veil between your world and the world of the gods," said Oxlac.

Luna turned to her Abuela Monze. "Can you please translate for me, abuela? I have no idea what he means."

"I'll try my best. You are, in a way, right. We are basically invisible. The gods of ancient Egypt live here and exist side by side with their worshipers, but their world is in the unseen and hidden from most humans."

Luna reached out to touch the unsuspecting gazelle. Her hand passed through the side of the animal as if she were a ghost. The gazelle looked up from its peaceful meal, interrupted by the sensation of Luna's unseen hand.

"Did it feel me?" Luna asked Oxlac.

"In a way," he replied.

"You're really confusing," said Luna.

"Oxlac enjoys being mysterious," smiled Abuela Monze as she took a drink of water from the animal skin pouch at her side. She handed it to Luna and said, "Take a drink. It's hot here." The fresh, cool water was so inviting, Luna took several gulps before she felt satisfied.

"The sun is setting," said Freya. "Let us leave. I imagine the night brings more dangers."

"Well, then, let's see what creature awaits us," said Athena as she casually drew her sword as one would with an umbrella if expecting rain.

"Wait," interjected Luna. "Take your shield, Athena. Whatever it is, there are a lot of them," said Luna.

Athena turned to Freya for an explanation.

"Do as she says," said Freya. "Luna has not failed us yet."

Athena's tall, sleek frame grew rigid as she advanced toward the long, slender boat. Freya followed at Athena's side. Oxlac pulled an obsidian axe from his medicine bag and motioned for Luna and Monze to stay behind him. Before Athena could reach the water's edge, the head of a cobra snake rose swiftly from the water. Its brown and black head was the size of an alligator's snout. It struck fiercely at Athena. She lifted her shield in time to thwart the snake's sword-length fangs. In the same moment, another snake sprang from the water and struck at Freya. She was knocked to the hard, parched earth, and scrambled to use her magic just in time to freeze the snake in mid bite, only inches from her face.

Luna noticed the snakes' bodies remained in the water, as if their tails were tied down to the river bed. She was about to tell this to Oxlac when she heard a familiar, resounding sound. The shaman blew another mighty breath into his shell. Luna screamed as three more snakes leapt forward, snapping viciously at Athena and Freya. Oxlac lunged forward and swung his ax, striking each of the enormous cobras.

"Did he call for help?" screamed Luna to her abuela.

"Yes, but I don't know if he will come," answered Abuela Monze as she pulled Luna away from the river.

Several more cobras emerged from the water and it seemed impossible they would ever reach the canoe, which bobbed gently on the chaotic water only a few feet away. A dark figure drew Luna's attention to the middle of the river. Luna could not discern if the figure she saw was human or not. She was only sure that it was tall and as black as onyx. The figure stood in the center of a vessel the size of a small ship. A white vulture perched on the bow of the vessel. The slender boat cut through the water rapidly, but there appeared to be no one rowing. As the dark figure approached, Luna recognized one of her favorite Egyptian gods.

"Anubis," she whispered to herself in disbelief.

Anubis lifted his hand in a silent command. The snakes unanimously desisted their attack and retreated to the depths of the river.

"I can't believe he came," said Abuela Monze with relief.

"You mean he would have normally just left us to die?" asked Luna.

"He is bound to his duties," answered Abuela Monze.

Anubis interjected with a growl-like bark.

"What did he say?" asked Luna.

"We are lucky. It is his lunch break," replied Oxlac matter-of-factly. Luna could not decide if Oxlac was kidding or not.

Athena and Freya observed Anubis and exchanged subtle looks of approval. His canine head and human body were almost as striking as his skin, which shone like black marble. His towering height was accentuated by a muscular build. He wore long, gold cuffs on his wrists and ankles. A thick, golden ankh rested on a necklace against his bare chest and he held a long metal staff in his left hand.

"I have the impression he would make a challenging opponent," said Athena.

"A formidable impression, to be sure," agreed Freya.

The boat approached slowly and came to a gentle stop at the shore. With the retreat of the slithery assailants, the wild waters were calm and the sounds of the river filled Luna's ears once more. The piercing cry of a bird overhead broke the spell Anubis held over the group as he stood calmly, waiting for Luna and the others. Oxlac bowed his head in greeting and climbed aboard the boat with the kind of agility that only comes with the experience of climbing into various vessels in strange lands.

Luna scrambled aboard, eager for a close-up view of Anubis, guardian of the dead. The ancient god turned slowly to look down at Luna. Her eyes followed the path along Anubis' snout and stopped at his intense, dark eyes. Anubis huffed forcefully through his snout, causing Luna to jump with a start. Oxlac chuckled discreetly. Luna would have chastised him had she not been so pleased at finally seeing the shaman smile.

~

As they travelled along the river, Luna stood closely to Anubis. She eagerly tapped his shoulder. He turned to look down at her with a hint of impatience in his eyes. Luna had to strain her neck to make eye contact. She wished he would at least bend forward to lessen his height and allow for easier conversation.

"So, you measure people's hearts after they die?" asked Luna. Anubis huffed and nodded his dog-shaped head.

"So, do most people make it, or do they get eaten by the hippopotamus?" Luna was giddy with disbelief at having a conversation with, in her opinion, a celebrity.

Anubis replied with a growl-like bark.

"He says, let us measure your heart and see," said Oxlac.

Luna quickly hid behind Abuela Monze who turned to Anubis. "It would surely be lighter than your feather," rebuffed

Monze. She was not particularly fond of anyone teasing her granddaughter. Athena and Freya kept their eyes on the peaceful river and pretended not to be amused at Luna's expense. They knew better than to offend Monze.

As they glided up the river, the activity along the water increased. Various ships from small to large were sprawled across the water. Some were stopped on the river banks, stocked with goods and animals to be sold. There were countless people in the midst of their merchant lives. Some sold their goods from their boats to awaiting customers on the shore. Others unloaded their glass beads, vegetables, or livestock onto carts to be traded in the city center.

Luna noticed almost every person wore thick, black liner around their eyes. "Everyone really does wear kohl," said Luna. Freya and Athena looked to Oxlac for an answer. He motioned to his eyes, mimicking an outline.

The jewelry alone easily announced the status of each individual. The upper-class men and women wore amulets and bracelets of gold. Their collars were lined with colorful beads, and some even boasted precious jewels. Servants in plain linen gowns followed behind their wealthy masters and hauled about their purchases in obedient silence.

As Luna and the other's rode along the center of the river observing the unsuspecting inhabitants, Luna was drawn to a curious sight. A woman of obvious elevated rank bartered passionately with a merchant while her young daughter, not more than five years old, stared in wonder at the sunlight sparkling on the water's surface. The erratic bursts of bright lights danced about her smiling face. She held a small, wooden horse close to her chest as if she dared not lose such a precious toy. The young girl then lifted her head and locked eyes with Luna. She waved at Luna as the boat glided away.

"She saw me," exclaimed Luna.

"Many children see through the veil," said Abuela Monze.

"How?" asked Luna.

"They are fresh from The Creator," answered Oxlac.

"I think I get what you mean. It's like how people say animals can see ghosts," said Luna.

"Something like that," said Abuela Monze.

Luna's stomach began to rumble as she stared longingly at the various foods aboard the merchant ships. "I am very hungry, Abuela," she said to Monze. Oxlac motioned for Anubis to move toward a nearby vessel. Oxlac reached over for a basket of figs and plums on a merchant's small boat. He handed the basket to Luna.

"We have to pay for this, Oxlac. Just because they can't see us doesn't mean we should steal," said Luna.

Oxlac hesitated as they were already pressed for time.

"We should do the right thing, even if they can't see us," urged Luna.

Oxlac sighed and reached into the small pouch still hanging from his neck. He pulled out a gold coin and reached over to the merchant's boat to place it where the fruit basket had been. Luna beamed with gratitude and satisfaction that the shaman had respected her request. Oxlac patted Luna on the head. "You are a good little rat," he said tenderly.

Luna picked up a fig from the basket and took in the sweet aroma. She could not remember a fruit ever smelling so heavenly. She gently pried open the soft flesh and bit into its luscious center. The others, tempted by Luna's enjoyment, bit into the fruits as well, except for Anubis, who kept his eyes on the river. The contents of the basket were swiftly devoured, and before the group realized, they felt the vessel slow as it reached the shallow sand of the shore.

When Luna looked up, she saw they were at the foot of a temple covered in paintings of Isis and Osiris. The entrance was guarded by pillars shaped like Anubis. Luna was immediately captivated. She turned to Anubis. "You are one of my favorites," she said with an overflowing tone of admiration. Though his face did not move, Luna could see a softening in his eyes and she knew he was flattered.

Anubis led them into the temple. As they followed in silence, Oxlac whispered to Monze, who then whispered to Luna: "Mija, we must accompany Anubis on his, umm, duties before seeing Isis,"

Abuela Monze said with hushed urgency. "Please try not to be terrified."

Luna barely heard the words. Her eyes were fixated on the intricacy of the colorful hieroglyphs which adorned every inch of the interior walls. An intoxicating scent permeated the air. Luna scanned for its origin and spotted small triangle-shaped incense burning throughout each room they passed.

"Do you know Isis, abuela?" asked Luna.

"I do."

"How did you meet her? Why did you meet her?"

"Oxlac and I helped her find her husband's body."

Luna's eyes widened with amazement. "You helped save Osiris?" Abuela Monze nodded with a smile.

"Was it an adventure, like this one?"

"I almost died, and Grandpa forbid me to leave with Oxlac again."

The group came to a halt.

"I believe we have arrived," said Freya.

"This is unexpected. I imagined a dreary place for his morbid tasks," said Athena as she surveyed the lush, bright surroundings. Luna would never have imagined Anubis to judge the recently deceased in a picturesque garden. Brilliant rays from the sun cascaded down through the open ceiling, illuminating exotic plants and flowers Luna imagined only grew for Isis. Several hummingbirds hovered about the flowers, tenderly drinking their nectar. A low growl rumbled from Anubis.

"Flowers please him," said Oxlac, translating for Anubis.

"He's joking, right?" Luna asked Athena.

"I can never tell," replied Athena.

At the center of the garden was a large pond. To one side of it stood a small wooden table that held a simple golden scale. It looked to Luna like a cross with a small basket on either end. In one of the baskets sat a single white feather. Anubis took the feather and handed it to Luna.

"For the good little rat," Anubis whispered in Luna's ear.

"You talked," shouted Luna. "But how did you do that? Your mouth didn't move." Luna turned excitedly to the others. "He gave me his feather," Luna whispered in disbelief. She carefully tucked the long feather into her back pocket, hoping it would not be ruined during the remainder of their journey.

"It is because you are easy to love, little Luna," said Freya.

"I can agree to that. And I am not often fond of humans or gods," said Athena.

Anubis barked a loud call. The same white vulture from the river swooped in through the ceiling and landed with the grace of experience on Anubis' forearm. Anubis carefully removed a feather from the vulture and placed it on one side of the scale. There it sat, waiting patiently for its next customer. The vulture then took flight to another room in the temple.

The water in the pond began to bubble, and through it a sarcophagus emerged. It floated, as if by force, toward Anubis. He waited at the edge of the pond as the sarcophagus stopped at the pond's edge. Anubis uncovered the stone coffin and out stepped a slender man with an aged, sour face, dressed in a fine linen tunic. The man stepped dutifully toward the table and handed Anubis a small clay jar. From the jar, Anubis removed the man's heart and placed it on the scale, opposite the white feather. Luna assumed the man's heart would be lighter than the feather and they would be on their way to Isis, but she was wrong. The unworthy weight of the man's heart caused the scale to tilt unfavorably. Luna's stomach dropped. She hoped the consequences were not true to her grandmother's stories of Anubis. Once again, she was wrong. The water in the pond began to bubble, but before Luna could behold the outcome of the man's fate, her abuela swiftly turned Luna away and all she could hear were the terrified screams of the man. She was relieved to be spared the memory of a hippopotamus monster devouring a man. She was even more relieved to not live in a time and place where it was possible to die twice.

"We go now," said Oxlac.

By the calm expression on their faces, Luna gathered this was not the first time her Abuela Monze and Oxlac had observed Anubis at work.

"I never wish to see that again. What a horrid creature," said Freya.

"I quite enjoyed it," said Athena with satisfaction. "And you, Luna, what did you think?"

"Abuela didn't let me see it," said Luna.

"That is unfortunate," replied Athena.

Anubis led Luna and the others to a simple chamber with two ornate chairs surrounded with large statues of sleek, regal cats. Before he turned to leave, Anubis reached for Luna's hand and placed a small glass figurine of a scorpion in the center of her palm.

Lamenting the thought of saying goodbye, Luna whispered a melancholy, "Thank you." Anubis bowed to Luna and returned to his eternal duties. Luna felt a tingling in her hand. She looked down to see the scorpion figurine come to life. Before she could scream with fright, Luna heard a small voice in her mind order her to be calm. She knew immediately the scorpion was speaking to her with telepathy.

The small creature crawled along her arm and grew in size as it reached her neck. The tail wrapped around Luna's neck until it rested along her collarbone like a necklace. When Luna touched the scorpion, it was once again as still as glass.

Luna turned her attention back to the small chamber. There, a woman stood in the center of the room with a peaceful smile on her face. Luna knew, without question, it was Isis. Her skin shone like painted gold. Her dress was a vibrant green with red beading. Her eyelids were painted purple, with a thick border of dark eye liner. Thick black braids hung loosely around her shoulders. The same white vulture rested on a perch and pruned its feathers with no notice of the visitors. Isis looked over Oxlac admiringly.

"You are always a sight to see, Oxlac," she said.

Oxlac took a feather from his headdress and offered it to Isis. She smiled with acceptance and placed it in a blue and yellow glass jar already filled with feathers from Oxlac. Isis bowed her head in greeting to Freya, Athena, Abuela Monze, and stopped when she saw Luna. She lowered her face to Luna's.

"You are a surprise. What a beauty you are," said Isis as she turned to Oxlac. "She has the gift of sight. Did you know this, Oxlac?"

Oxlac nodded yes.

"Why are you here, child?" asked Isis softly.

"Because you can bring people back from the dead," answered Luna.

"Not just anyone, child. The one I brought back is my love, my most cherished one."

"Won't you please help Coatlicue too? We can't let her die," pleaded Luna.

Isis turned to the shaman and asked, "Is this truly why you are here?"

Oxlac bowed his head and nodded yes, ever so slightly.

"I cannot save your earth goddess," said Isis with sympathy.

"Why not?" asked Luna sternly, forgetting to restrain her anger.

"Calm down, mija. You can't speak to Isis like that," said Abuela Monze.

"It's not fair," said Luna. Her voice began to shake. "How could we come all this way for her to say no?"

Luna looked to Freya and Athena for support, but their eyes were locked on someone or something behind her. The first thought Luna had was that a monster had broken into the palace, but to her surprise Oxlac and Abuela Monze bowed and stepped to one side as a man took slow, heavy steps toward Isis. As he passed Luna, she noticed chunks of his skin were missing throughout his body, exposing the bone. Luna covered her mouth so she would not shout in disgust. The man took Isis by the hand and escorted her to sit in one of the chairs. He settled slowly in the chair next to Isis, still holding her hand.

"As Oxlac and Monze already know, this is my husband, Osiris," said Isis.

Freya and Athena bowed their heads without taking their eyes off the god of the underworld. Even they were struck by the severity of his appearance. Osiris turned to look straight at Luna. The flesh was gone from his left eye, leaving his eyeball floating eerily in the socket. The flesh from half of his face was also missing, exposing one side of his cheekbone and several teeth. Luna forced herself to bow her head in greeting.

Isis turned to Luna. "You must understand, death has parted Osiris and I once. I cannot risk my life," said Isis.

"I swear, I will keep you safe," said Athena with a sincerity that surprised even herself.

"I have no doubt of your capability," said Isis. "Your violence is legendary. As is your magic," said Isis to Freya. "I pity your enemies. However, my place is here with Osiris."

Abuela Monze turned to Oxlac, but he only looked away.

"My grandmother and Oxlac risked their lives for you," said Luna. The sternness in her voice broke the sullen stillness. "If it weren't for them, Osiris wouldn't be sitting there holding your hand," said Luna. She held Isis with a steady gaze. The weight of her words filled the room with a powerful silence.

"You are a clever girl," Isis finally said.

"Clever little rat," Oxlac said quietly to himself with approval.

"Coatlicue has a baby in her belly. If you let her die, her baby will die too," said Luna, knowing well that Isis was the goddess of motherhood as well as magic.

Isis looked at her king. They exchanged an unspoken understanding. Isis rose to kiss Osiris on his forehead and whispered in his ear. The god of the underworld nodded his head and let go of his queen's hand. Luna watched the tender exchange with wonder. In those few moments she understood the great love between Osiris and Isis. Although, endearing as the exchange was, Luna could not imagine kissing someone with missing skin on their face. *Love is blind, but in a good way*, she thought to herself.

"Don't stare, mija, it's rude," whispered Abuela Monze.

"Of course I'm staring, abuela. The skin is missing from half his face and he's the god of the underworld. If this is the only time I'm going to be around Egyptian gods, I'm going to stare." Luna paused a moment and said, "Why does he look like that?"

"He was killed and Isis brought him back to life," answered Abuela Monze.

"I know that part, but are you sure she is the best person to bring someone back from the dead?" asked Luna. "He looks like a zombie."

"Trust me, mija," replied Abuela Monze. "She did her best, considering the condition he was found in. He was literally in pieces."

Osiris rose from his seat and stood next to Isis.

"He will open the door," said Isis.

By this point, Luna knew that any words spoken by these gods were laden with deeper meaning, and so she understood when Isis said door, she really meant a portal. Osiris turned to face the stone wall behind them and lifted his hand to trace the outline of a door in the air. As he did, the form of door took shape in the wall. He pushed open the door with an effortless touch. Luna peered through and found herself looking down a long, dark hallway. At the end of the hallway was a bright light. She heard the sounds of angry shouting in a language she could not understand.

CHAPTER 8

THE BATTLE

Trepidation guided each footstep as Luna and the others proceeded down the corridor. Luna turned back for a moment. She expected to see Osiris still standing at the opening of the portal, but now there was only darkness. Oxlac led the way, with Athena on guard at his side. Athena handed Oxlac Hades' helmet. "Keep it safe until I need it," she ordered.

Freya remained a few paces behind Luna and Abuela Monze. Luna looked over to see Freya smile at her reassuringly, but Luna was not convinced. There was hesitation and uncertainty in Freya's eyes, but not fear, which Luna admired. Luna did not bother to trouble her imagination with the possibilities of what they would encounter at the end of the passageway. By now she expected each destination to surpass the wonder and danger of the previous. Though she was unsure of what was to come, Luna knew, without a doubt, that she was no longer afraid, and was compelled to help Oxlac and her abuela accomplish what they had set out to do.

Luna covered her ears as the angry voices at the end of the passageway grew louder. The unpleasant volume reminded her of the shrill sound of passing ambulance sirens. Light from an unseen source at the end of the corridor began to illuminate the intricately carved walls. Luna recognized the ancient symbols of the Aztec language. The air suddenly felt humid and heavy with an intoxicating aroma.

"What is this scent?" asked Athena as she held her shield out before her in case of attack.

"Copal," replied Oxlac.

"Sacred incense," explained Abuela Monze.

They had reached the end of the corridor and were now standing in the center of an entryway to a room filled with giants.

"Malinche," hissed a creature Luna could never have imagined seeing with her own eyes. How many times had Luna and her Abuela Monze pored over books with stories and images of ancient Aztec gods? Their shapes and colors fascinated Luna. Luna often wondered, *who could have thought of such things*? Hybrid creatures with human bodies made of colorful skin, with claws for feet and eyes like animals.

"Malinche," repeated the towering creature. Its red flesh was covered in fractal patterns of yellow and white. It pointed a long, sharp finger at the round belly of what looked to be a human woman.

"What is it saying?" asked Luna in a cautious whisper.

"Traitor," answered Oxlac.

"Is that Coatlicue?" asked Luna of the pregnant woman, whose average height was dwarfed by the giant-sized figures surrounding her.

"Yes," whispered Oxlac.

"Who are the giants?" asked Luna.

"Gods," replied Oxlac.

The shouting continued.

"What are they saying, Oxlac?" asked Luna intently as she felt the rapid escalation of anger in the room. Oxlac took the small pouch from his necklace and shook out the last remnants of enchanted powder. He silently ordered his companions to form a small circle. He motioned for them to close their eyes. One by one, he blew a small bit of dust into their left ear. As soon as he did, Luna realized she was able to understand the words of the screaming gods, who had not yet noticed the newcomers.

"Majority rules. The traitor dies," hissed the same god with red skin. Several voices rose in agreement. Another figure stepped in closely, challenging the accuser. "You will not harm her," it growled back. Luna thought to herself it must be a female deity; the body was lean and feminine with enormous butterfly-like wings sprouting from its shoulders.

"Are these your gods, Oxlac?" asked Freya.

Oxlac simply nodded.

"What is the name of the one with wings?" asked Freya, relieved they had an ally.

"Itzpapalotl. She is the obsidian butterfly," answered Oxlac without taking his eyes off Coatlicue.

"Will she fight for us?" asked Athena, carefully scanning the room. "I am confident, but not foolish. Your gods are robust. More fighters would be helpful."

"Yes," replied Oxlac. He took a deep breath as if returning his mind to the present moment. He turned to Athena and Freya and said urgently, "You must keep us alive until Mictlantecuhtli comes."

Luna could not hear what was said after that. Her mind was with Coatlicue. Luna looked down at the space between the two gods. There Coatlicue stood and observed the debate with a solemn face. Luna was astounded by the fierce serenity and beauty of Coatlicue. The ill-fated goddess stood bravely and in silence as she awaited her sentence. It inspired in Luna much needed bravery, as she had not anticipated such adversaries.

Luna welcomed the sudden flood of courage and hoped she could transfer it to the shaman. She reached out and took Oxlac's hand. Not once, until that moment, had she seen Oxlac display any lack of valor; but when she looked up at him, she saw the pain of a worried heart.

Without warning, Oxlac turned Luna away from the commotion and held her tightly. Luna struggled to turn back and not lose sight of Coatlicue. She could hear the gasps of her companions. And then there was silence. When Oxlac finally released Luna, she turned to see Coatlicue's lifeless body on the floor and her head lying several feet away. Luna began to scream. It was a horror she had never felt in her life. Her abuela grabbed her by the shoulders to silence her, for all the gods how now turned their attention to the unwelcomed visitors. The pain in Luna immediately shifted to anger and she began to scream at the gods of Oxlac's land.

"How could you?" she cried. "You're evil. You are monsters," she howled.

One of the gods stepped forward and stooped to inspect Luna. Luna immediately recognized the features of a woman, but it was no human woman. She had eyes like a cat and claws for hands. Luna wanted to be repulsed, but the goddess reminded her of a striking jaguar.

"I am no monster. I am Coyolxauhqui and I have served justice," said the goddess.

Luna looked down at the long blade with dripping blood in Coyolxauhqui's hand.

"You killed your mother. You're evil," yelled Luna.

"I do not tolerate traitors. My mother made a child with a human. They are beneath us. She knew well the punishment was death. And if you insult me again, I will cut off your head as well."

Coyolxauhqui took a threatening step toward Luna. Athena lunged and struck Coyolxauhqui with her shield. Luna could feel Freya yanking her away from the sounds of Athena's swinging sword and clanging shield, but she held her eyes fast to Coatlicue's body. It slowly began to move, and then violently shake. Luna could see something forcing its way out of Coatlicue's open neck. It grew as it emerged, and within seconds a giant man with blue skin rose to his feet. He wore animal skins and held a shield and ax.

Athena fought ferociously, holding her own against the giant gods. As Oxlac was forbidden to harm any creature or god from his land, he wrapped his arms tightly around Luna and Abuela Monze. Freya had her back against Oxlac and held her arms out to create a shield around them. Several star gods struck at the invisible buffer as Freya struggled to hold them off.

Safe for the time being, Oxlac reached for his shell and blew a mighty breath. Luna covered her ears until the powerful sound subsided. She realized Isis was not with them and saw her hovering over Coatlicue's body, casting a spell of protection so it would not be trampled.

The giant man with blue skin jumped to Athena's aid. He was not as tall as the immortals, but easily knocked down several star gods and stabbed one in the heart, killing it instantly. Athena beheaded another and barely missed an ax as it swung close to her face. Athena and the blue-skinned man fought viciously. Like a choreographed dance, they would duck or jump with swift precision. The blue-skinned man would lift his shield and Athena would step from behind him and thrust her sword, each protecting the other with perfect timing. They were soon outnumbered.

Oxlac flung Hades helmet to Athena. The blue-skinned man watched Athena disappear as she lowered the helmet onto her head. The massive gods began dropping to the floor as they were struck by the unseen goddess of war.

Luna recoiled at the bloodbath. "Stop," she screamed. "Stop fighting," she sobbed angrily. Overcome, Luna pushed past Freya and stood looking up at a snarling star god. Before she could think, her necklace moved. The star god lifted its dagger and aimed for Luna. Before anyone could react, the scorpion around Luna's neck jumped to the floor and lifted its tail. In mid swing, the scorpion grew twice the size of the god and brought down its massive tail. The star god was knocked to the floor. The scorpion swung its tail again and took out more than half of the assailants.

Athena and the blue-skinned man paused as they noticed the myriad of flying bodies. The scorpion pointed its sharp tail at the remaining gods until they lowered their weapons in submission. The scorpion moved toward Luna and protectively wrapped its tail around her.

Athena removed the helmet and took advantage of the calm moment to catch her breath and nod her head with thanks to her new companion. Now that they were still, Athena could see the blue-skinned man had a large black stripe across his eyes like a mask. The rest of his face was covered with a horizontal orange stripe.

"What are you called?" asked Athena.

"Huitzilopochtli," answered the blue-skinned man with a forced whisper, as if he was unsure of his ability to speak.

Coyolxauhqui stepped forward. She was the most human looking, and the resemblance to her mother, Coatlicue, was not difficult to see. Athena had spent most of the battle against Coyolxauhqui, but understood the invitation to fight in that moment was not for her. The blue-skinned man turned to accept the challenge.

"You were made in sin and must die," whispered Coyolxauhqui without a hint of regret.

There was no great struggle between brother and sister. Without warning and without a word, Huitzilopochtli beheaded her with uncanny speed.

"Why are you killing your family?" Luna screamed at the blue-skinned man and the other gods who remained living.

Adrenaline and fear rushed through her body as she trembled from seeing such violence.

"They killed my mother," said Huitzilopochtli. He held Luna in a steady gaze, speaking to her with his eyes. Though she did not agree with his act of revenge, she understood his reason.

There was an eerie stillness as Luna noticed every god retreating from the center of the room.

"Mictlantecuhtli is here," they whispered.

Luna could hear a strangely loud echo of bare feet approaching as a new creature appeared. It looked like a sickly, skinny human with painted white skin and a skeleton head. The feet were human, but it had claws for hands. Its eyes, gums, and hanging tongue were a deep, blood red. It wore a sinister smile that was made all the more ghoulish by its jagged teeth. It was covered in circular designs of yellow and blue from head to toe.

Mictlantecuhtli approached Luna's scorpion without hesitation. The scorpion lowered its tail and froze as if in a trance. Mictlantecuhtli touched the scorpion lightly on one of its legs. It sank to the floor and returned to its necklace form.

"Did you kill it?" asked Luna angrily.

Mictlantecuhtli smiled and whispered, "Shhh. Your pet is asleep now."

Luna swiftly grabbed her necklace from the floor and replaced it around her neck.

"You called me, Oxlac? What's all the fuss about?" asked Mictlantecuhtli, completely oblivious or without concern of the corpses in the room. Oxlac bowed before the skeleton-like creature.

"I beg for your permission to revive Coatlicue," the shaman asked with grave sincerity.

Abuela Monze cleared her throat and steadied her words. "She has been punished. She was killed, as was ordered by the others. Now, if you return her, she will be free of her crime. She deserves to live again."

"But her head is gone. She'll be a bore," Mictlantecuhtli giggled.

Luna was appalled by the distasteful humor, as were her companions, who grimaced with abhorrence, except Oxlac, who looked to have expected such a reply.

"What if we can fix her head and bring her back to life?" asked Luna. Her mind searched frantically for the right words to lure Mictlantecuhtli in their favor. Luna knew if Oxlac had called the skeleton monster, then it must be someone who could help. Her voice shook with hesitation as her throat began to close with fear. If Mictlantecuhtli refused, all would be lost. Luna noticed a restriction in her lungs. The air grew thinner with each moment Mictlantecuhtli was in the room.

"You know magic?" asked Mictlantecuhtli with enthusiastic curiosity.

"My abuela and her friends do," Luna answered. She kept her gaze to the ground to avoid the skeleton creature's wild red eyes.

"If you can pull her spirit from the underworld and fix her head, you can keep her," Mictlantecuhtli said, and clapped its hands with excitement. "What is your name, human girl?" Mictlantecuhtli inquired with a sinister grin.

"Luna."

"And what does that mean?" asked Mictlantecuhtli, as it stepped toward Luna.

"Moon," answered Luna as she tried to ignore the feeling of her body freezing in fear. She was sure her olive skin had turned pale. Luna discreetly held her breath. Mictlantecuhtli smelled like burning firewood and blood.

"What is a moon, girl?"

"Like the moon in the sky that shines at night."

"We do not have a moon," whispered Mictlantecuhtli.

"It is like a sun for night-time," said Luna in a tone she had heard parents use to show their children something new.

Satisfied, Mictlantecuhtli addressed the other gods in the room. "I see you hiding back there. What do you say? Shall we give them a chance? Say, I."

"I," said the sun god Tonatiuh. Several more "I's" echoed from the other gods, though a few remained stoic in their obstinacy.

"Okie dokie," said Mictlantecuhtli.

"That's it? That easy?" asked Luna.

"Yes," replied Mictlantecuhtli with an innocent grin.

"I don't understand. Every other god has been so difficult."

"Because I am bored," answered Mictlantecuhtli with a sigh. "I wake up, take some souls. Have breakfast and take more souls. Take a nap and then more souls. Same thing, over and over again." Mictlantecuhtli whispered with feverish giggles, "Sometimes, for fun, I take a man's soul but quickly return it. He gets really dizzy and falls down."

"That's not funny," said Luna with disgust.

"It is very funny to me," replied Mictlantecuhtli with delight.

Luna could not decide what was more disturbing about Mictlantecuhtli, the jagged teeth against red gums or its sense of humor.

Oxlac carried Coatlicue's body and laid her before Mictlantecuhtli. Isis rested Coatlicue's dismembered head against the open wound between her shoulders. Freya and Abuela Monze knelt at either side of Isis. Freya removed her sacred necklace and rested it upon the wound across the earth goddess' neck. Isis took the emerald scarab beetle from the center of her crown and placed it on the center of Freya's necklace.

Luna wanted to look away and avoid the unpleasant sight, but she knew if she did, she would miss the opportunity to witness a miracle from the finest magic at work. Abuela Monze and Freya bowed their heads in concentration and held tightly to Coatlicue's shoulders. Isis chanted until the necklace began to glow. When Isis placed her hands on the necklace, a wave of energy passed through the room. A yellow ball of light burst forth, as if a candle had been lit over Coatlicue's body. As Isis continued her chants, the light grew to a blinding brightness and lowered into the lifeless body. Coatlicue's eyes shot open and she took in a long, deep breath.

"Wonderful, just wonderful," Mictlantecuhtli exclaimed and clapped its hands vigorously. "You have put on an amusing show."

"Do you promise you will allow her to live?" asked Isis through clenched teeth. "I know who you are and the fondness you have for collecting souls," said the goddess of the underworld.

"Let's toss a coin over it," replied Mictlantecuhtli. Abuela Monze and Luna gasped.

"Kidding, just kidding," said Mictlantecuhtli through bursts of giddy laughter. The skeleton creature dabbed at the tears in its eyes and finally said, "Since you've put me in a good mood, Coatlicue will live and you may return home."

"Wait," said Coatlicue in a weak whisper. She rose to her feet with the aid of Freya and Oxlac. "I want my children to live. Please have mercy on them and restore their lives," said Coatlicue as she looked at all of the perished bodies surrounding them.

"Even the very naughty one?" asked Mictlantecuhtli with a quizzical grin.

"Yes. Even she."

Mictlantecuhtli took a deep breath and sighed, "Sure, why not."

The dead bodies sprang to life simultaneously, except for Coyolxauhqui. Mictlantecuhtli picked up her decapitated head and patted it. "I have special plans for you," it whispered. Luna turned away at the macabre sight. Every mortal and immortal being in the room held their breath. Luna saw the muscles in Oxlac's jaw tighten with anticipation of the next few moments.

"Mercy for the family that killed you. You are uncommonly kind," said Mictlantecuhtli to Coatlicue. "Now I am impressed and surprised. I think you deserve a little reward, so I will do something kind for your unruly daughter that I think you will appreciate."

Coatlicue stepped away nervously, unsure of her safety.

Mictlantecuhtli spoke with exaggerated authority: "Coatlicue will be allowed to live in peace atop the sacred mountain with her human. I know it will bother the others, and I like to make people grumpy."

Mictlantecuhtli drummed its bony fingers together in thought and finally said, "We will forgive the naughty Coyolxauhqui. From this day on, she will shine down on her mother each night. A few days of the year she will be allowed to visit her mother in the temple, and on those nights only the stars will shine in the sky. She will be our moon." Mictlantecuhtli, quite pleased, smiled at Luna. She did her best to smile back and not squirm at its black, sharp teeth.

"And my son?" asked Coatlicue.

"Oh yes. We cannot forget our new blue friend. I think he would make a suitable god of war. He will share the day sky with the sun god, Tonatiuh. Probably best to keep these siblings apart. Which reminds me…"

Mictlantecuhtli gestured for the blue-skinned man to take his sister's head, and motioned for him to swing it up and through the skylight. Luna watched as Coyolxauhqui's head flew through the firmament until it landed high above them. Luna could clearly see the shape of a woman's face in the pale white disc. She stood in awe, taking in the realization she had just witnessed the creation of the moon.

Luna drew close to Mictlantecuhtli. "You have a good heart," said a surprised Luna. "Who are you?"

"Mictlantecuhtli," said the white-skinned creature as it leaned in closely to Luna. Luna began to see a ball of light leaving her body and pulling towards Mictlantecuhtli. Oxlac yanked her away and her soul snapped back into her body.

"God of death," whispered Oxlac to Luna.

"Oh," said Luna, as she took a few steps back towards the safety of her Abuela Monze. *You might even scare Hades*, thought Luna. "Thank you," she whispered to Mictlantecuhtli from a safe distance as the heaviness in her heart renewed with joy and relief for Coatlicue's deliverance.

"Is it a boy or a girl?" Luna asked her abuela, trying not to gesture at the god of death.

"Neither," Abuela Monze answered.

Mictlantecuhtli stepped in closely to the group. "I am very impressed. What a good show. May I kiss your hands please, to say thank you and goodbye?"

Freya held out her hand as if it was too close to a fire and pulled it away quickly. Mictlantecuhtli's small kiss caused half of her soul to pull away from her body momentarily. Athena was next. The god of death smiled mischievously. "You are a wonderful fighter. You have killed so much, you could be Mictlantecuhtli." The god of death squealed with delight and said, "Do you get it? You could be me?"

"Very humorous," responded Athena cautiously as she focused on not having her soul sucked away when Mictlantecuhtli kissed her hand.

Abuela Monze held out her shaky hand with her eyes closed. Mictlantecuhtli laughed and smacked it away playfully. The god of death turned to Oxlac with open arms. "A hug, Oxlac?" it asked. The shaman declined the precarious gesture of affection with a courteous shake of his head. Mictlantecuhtli approached Isis. She did not flinch as the god of death leaned in, nor did a speck of her soul leave her body.

"Do you know how often it is someone impresses me?" asked the god of death in an unnerving whisper.

"I do not know," replied Isis with apprehension. Mictlantecuhtli's sense of humor was nothing short of suspenseful.

"Never," said Mictlantecuhtli in a hushed voice. "Never, never, never," repeated the god of death in a burst of anger. Mictlantecuhtli took a deep breath. "So, because you have pleased me, I will give you a gift," it said cheerfully.

Isis tried to step away, but Mictlantecuhtli grabbed her by the arm and whispered, "You will not fear death again, not even from me." In the place where Isis had removed the scarab from her crown, the god of death made a fist. Its long nails sank deeply and created a flow of crimson, which formed a large red circle in the middle of her crown. Her golden skin began to sparkle.

"You feel good, yes?" asked the god of death.

"Wonderful," said the goddess as she laughed and stifled tears at once.

"Eternal life. My gift to you," proclaimed Mictlantecuhtli proudly.

The god of death stood quietly for a few moments as everyone braced themselves for the unexpected.

"Bye-bye," said Mictlantecuhtli nonchalantly, and turned to leave. The echo of its bare feet against the temple floor faded to silence and the atmosphere in the room suddenly felt light.

Appeased, and some bored by the resolution, most of the onlooking gods left the temple. The revived star gods fled to the furthest corners of the sky.

As a gesture of peace, the blue-skinned man took Coyolxauhqui's lifeless body, and placed it on the last step of the temple. The sun's rays transformed her body to stone, and sealed her figure inside the shape of a great disc. Now that Coyolxauhqui was a moon goddess she would no longer need her bodily form.

When Coatlicue turned to face Luna, she understood Oxlac's tenacious efforts to save his earth goddess. Upon meeting her gaze, Luna's heart filled with devotion and melted with love. Luna and the others stood transfixed. The innocent beauty of Coatlicue was powerfully disarming.

Coatlicue embraced each one of her saviors. Luna felt the most wonderful sensation of incandescent love at Coatlicue's touch.

Coatlicue caressed the necklace that now lay across her scarred neck. She turned to Freya. "This belonged to you?" asked Coatlicue with tenderness.

"Yes," answered Freya.

"You must allow me to replace it," said Coatlicue.

Coatlicue removed a golden bracelet from her wrist. Without effort, she stretched open the bracelet until it was the shape of a beautiful necklace filled with colorful gems. Coatlicue placed the necklace on Freya and said, "You will shed no more tears. This necklace will lead you to your husband."

Freya could not speak. She turned to Oxlac, her wide eyes full of amazement. Oxlac smiled.

"What are they talking about, abuela? asked Luna, completely bewildered. "Freya lost her husband?"

"I will tell you the story when we get home," Abuela Monze said and kissed Luna on her forehead.

Coatlicue reached for Oxlac and held him tightly, her gratitude brimming over. She took the pouch from his necklace and gently blew into the opening. She closed the small bag with a knowing smile.

"More magic," said Oxlac to Luna, who had been observing the exchange.

Oxlac blew a mighty breath into his conch shell. A flurry of hummingbirds arrived from every direction of the temple and flew in circles until three small hurricanes formed.

"Your way home," said Oxlac to his companions.

"Don't we need four?" asked Luna.

"Oxlac knows me well enough to anticipate my desire to return with Athena and retrieve my cloak," said Freya. "With it, I can return home from anywhere."

Though eager to return home, Luna was filled with a melancholy reluctance to leave her friends she had unexpectedly become attached to. She forced herself to step forward and say goodbye.

"No need, little rat, we will see each other again," said Athena.

The blue-skinned Huitzilopochtli approached Athena and offered his shield. "I am honored," she said, and handed the god of war her shield in return. Without another word, Athena stepped through the portal with Freya and vanished. Isis bowed to Oxlac and Monze. She turned to Luna and smiled as she stepped through the portal. Luna felt a pang of sadness as she watched them disappear.

"Our turn," said Abuela Monze. Her voice echoed in the quiet temple.

Luna took one last look at Coatlicue and felt a deep satisfaction. Oxlac took Luna and Monze by the hand and guided them through the whirling hummingbirds. Luna felt the rush of their soft feathers and then the softness of cold leaves. She opened her eyes to see Oxlac climbing down her orange tree. He lowered Luna and her grandmother gently onto the dewy grass. It was almost dawn.

Pink and orange clouds colored the sky and ushered in the new morning.

CHAPTER 9

HOME

Luna's father, Luis, shuffled into the kitchen, his hunger having roused him from a strangely deep sleep. As he lifted the lid of the pastry dish, the back door opened and in walked Luna and Abuela Monze in what he thought to be odd nightgowns.

"What are you doing in the backyard so early?" he asked, while still reaching for a sweet bread. Luna and her Abuela mumbled their apologies and headed straight for the bedrooms. Luis felt a cold breeze from the open door.

"At least close the door," he ordered.

"Close the door, Oxlac," shouted Luna from down the hall.

Luis turned to see a figure tuck below the doorframe and casually enter the kitchen. He dropped his pastry and fell back against the counter in fright.

"Good morning," said Oxlac as politely as possible and continued down the hall.

Dumbfounded, Luis observed as a turquoise feather fell from Oxlac's headdress and landed next to the pastry dish.

CHAPTER 10

ETERNAL LOVE

The Poet sat waiting in the jungle. Night had slowly given way to morning. Although the time transpired painfully, The Poet was prepared to remain in the jungle until Coatlicue returned. He refused the usual assistance of his servants and only requested food and water be brought to him. As he waited, poem after poem filled his heart. He saved each one carefully in memory in hopes to recite them to Coatlicue once they were reunited.

The Poet watched the shadows of the trees crawl across the jungle floor as morning blended into afternoon. Just as the sunlight began to sink below the trees, The Poet looked up from his thoughts to see a hummingbird had appeared and with it, the staircase. He jumped to his feet and raced up the stairs, with the hummingbird leading him.

The Poet reached the top and froze in disbelief when he saw Coatlicue at the entrance of the temple, as if waiting for him. The Poet knew from the smile on her peaceful face that she would not disappear from him again. As he rushed to Coatlicue, the staircase disappeared. It would no longer be needed.

~

And so it was, each night Coatlicue greeted her daughter, the moon, with a silence filled with a mother's devotion. As Coatlicue sat under the glorious illumination of Coyolxauhqui, The Poet would whisper tender hymns of adoration and affection to his love, rapturous verses for only the earth goddess to hear. Words that would have ensured The Poet's lifelong fame and beyond had he chosen to remain in the human world. But what would that have been compared to eternity with his beloved?

And there, in the temple atop the sacred mountain, Coatlicue and her poet would remain for all time, with no one to disturb them in the gentle fervor of their love.

UNTIL NEXT TIME....

Acknowledgments

I must first thank my friend and brilliant writing mentor, Jakob Austin Burgos, who dedicated so much of his time and wisdom to helping me bring this story to fruition and inspired me to grow as a writer. I also wish to thank my dear friends Elizabeth Santana, Stephanie Fastro and Veronica Lopez for their feedback and support. A heartfelt thank you to Henrik Rosenborg for the unique and beautiful cover art. Most of all, I wish to thank my beloved family, especially my children, for the joy their love brings to my life.

Made in the USA
Middletown, DE
23 April 2023

29332520R00080